FAIL TO SEE

"Their vision of me never mattered;
they could only judge my
surface, never the gold buried in my soul."

AMBER WESTBROOKS

Copyright © 2026 Amber Westbrooks.

All rights reserved. No part of this book may be reproduced, stored, or transmitted by any means—whether auditory, graphic, mechanical, or electronic—without written permission of both publisher and author, except in the case of brief excerpts used in critical articles and reviews. Unauthorized reproduction of any part of this work is illegal and is punishable by law.

This story is a work of fiction drawn from truth. While inspired by real experiences, all names, places, and certain details have been changed to protect privacy and deepen the storytelling.

CONTENTS

Dedication v
Prologue vii

Chapter 1   What's My Name? 1
Chapter 2   The Early Years 10
Chapter 3   The shift 22
Chapter 4   Cycles & Survival 39
Chapter 5   When Innocence Was Interrupted 48
Chapter 6   Seeing It for What It Was 59
Chapter 7   When It All Fell Apart 69
Chapter 8   Life Be Life'n 84
Chapter 9   Emotional Roller-Coaster 90
Chapter 10   Motherhood & Mayhem 110
Chapter 11   Letting Go to Grow 117
Chapter 12   Healing Ain't Pretty But It's Necessary 126
Chapter 13   Amber's Crown 138
Chapter 14   This Is Who I Am 162
Chapter 15   Bloodlines & Battle Wounds 168
Chapter 16   Trauma survival 175
Chapter 17   Badges & Accusations 178
Chapter 18   The Hustle Plus The Calling 182
Chapter 19   Becoming The Woman I Prayed For 186

Epilogue 189
Reflection Letter 193
Acknowledgments 195
About the Author 197

DEDICATION

This book is dedicated to the forgotten, the misunderstood, the broken, and the brave.

To the young girls growing up too fast and walking through trauma with no blueprint.

To the teenagers and women who've been silenced by sexual assault, abuse, or neglect.

To the people dealing with sexually transmitted diseases, you are still worthy of love.

To those who've had to raise themselves, carry family burdens, or survive when love wasn't there.

To the mamas doing it alone with babies on your hips and tears in your eyes.

To the ones who had to choose between feeding your kids or feeding your dreams.

To the women who stayed, left, returned, and finally walked away for real this time.

To the ones fighting anxiety, depression, and invisible battles while still getting up every morning.

To anyone who's ever looked in the mirror and didn't recognize themselves but kept going anyway.

To the homeless, the hustlers, the healers, and the hopeful.

To the believers who lost their faith and the ones still praying through the pain.

To the women who've been on the blade, in the club, or in the system—your story doesn't end there.

To the LGBTQ+ community, especially those who never felt seen in their own skin.

To the ones who never had support but found strength in their chosen family.

To every entrepreneur grinding with no investors or no connections but still making it happen.

To every dreamer whose past tried to disqualify their future—this is for you.

And to the woman I used to be…

I see you. I love you. I forgive you.

This is more than a book.

This is a mirror, a message, and a movement.

You are not alone.

You are not what they called you.

You are more than what happened to you.

Keep going. Keep healing. Keep building.

You got this.

Amber Crown

PROLOGUE

This is my truth told through a story. The events in this book are etched into my soul. They shaped me, tested me, and pushed me to the edge of who I thought I was. Some details, names, and places have been changed, but the pain, the lessons, the journey—that's all real. Amber Crown is me.

A young, Black girl finding her voice in a world that tried to name her before she even knew who she was.

But she's not just me.

She's every person who's ever had to fight to reclaim their identity. Every soul that's ever felt unseen, unheard, or misunderstood. Amber is a reflection a mirror held up to anyone who's ever been told they weren't enough and decided to rise anyway. This book isn't just a collection of memories.

It's a journey. A walk through the moments that broke me.

The relationships that tested me.

The decisions that nearly destroyed me and the ones that saved me. It's about survival.

About carrying pain without letting it consume you.

About falling apart in silence and still managing to pull yourself together louder than the world expected. Even in the darkest places, I found light.

Even when I didn't recognize myself, I learned how to come home to who I really am. To the children, teens, men, and women who feel invisible:

You are not alone.

Your voice matters.

Your pain is valid.

Your healing is possible.

I know because I've lived it. I've carried the weight of disappointment; felt the sting of betrayal.

Sat with the kind of heartbreak that doesn't have words.

I've fought battles no one could see with scars I didn't even know how to explain. But I also found strength in places I didn't think strength could survive.

And eventually, I found myself. Let me say this to you now whoever you are, wherever you are: You don't need permission to heal.

You don't have to wait for someone to believe in you to rise.

You don't owe anyone your silence.

And you don't have to carry shame for things you never asked to survive. No one gets to define you but you.

The world will try.

It will hand you labels, boxes, trauma, and expectations.

But only you hold the truth of who you are.

You are enough. You are worthy. You are unstoppable.

This is my story.

But maybe, in some way, it's yours too.

Amber Crown.

CHAPTER ONE

WHAT'S MY NAME?

Finding power in identity when the world tried to rename me

My name is Amber Crown. Born on October 21, 1991, in Oakland, California; a city that raised me with tough love and sharp lessons. I'm 34 now. A mother of three beautiful kids: two strong, smart girls twelve and eight and a five-year-old son who keeps me moving, smiling, and grounded. No village. My mother gave me to my father as an infant and my father and I have an estranged relationship, we always have…. I had to create my own tribe.

Right now? I'm on the grind. I attend The University of Texas at Austin, on my way to a master's degree in human sciences with a minor in human development and family studies. Come spring 2026, I'll be walkin' that stage and be one step closer to what sets my soul on fire: helping people heal, understand, and grow through the same storms I've had to fight my whole life.

But don't get it twisted.

I'm more than a mother.

More than a student.

More than another girl who "made it out."

I'm a survivor. A hustler. A visionary. A boss in the making.

A woman who's been to the bottom but never unpacked there.

Back in 2018 before degrees, before titles, before life started blooming again, I gave birth to an idea. A spark. A dream that would become my clothing line—Modest Royalteez... I didn't want to just sell shirts and hoodies. I wanted to thread *testimony* into every stitch. My clothes had to speak like I couldn't at first. They needed to say, "I've been through it, but I came out shining."

That brand reflected me: humbled, broken, refined, and rebuilt.

Then came 2020.

The world was on fire.

Pandemic. Panic. Pain.

And there I was—pregnant, broke, exhausted—watching life steadily movin' while I felt frozen.

I remember sittin' on the edge of my bed, belly full of my son, tears heavy in my eyes. I whispered to myself, "This is it. It's time."

That moment changed everything.

No savings. No mentors. No blueprint.

Just me, my faith, and my fire.

Brick by brick. Day by day.

I built my life back through every silent breakdown and late-night prayer. When I moved to Austin, TX in December of 2020, I just had my third child—a son. I still had a lot of pain from givin' birth and movin' to a new state with my little family. I liked Texas because it was a different feel and vibe my family needed.

I started my classes again in the spring as an online student and after I recovered for a month and a half I found a job. I was super busy around this time while everything in the world was shut down but work.

We experienced our first historic winter storm! We're not from a place where hurricanes and winter storms happen and let me tell you, it was HORRIFIC and TERRIFYING! My girls and my baby daddy were a nervous wreck. We barely had resources; the storm knocked the water out for 4 days. It was 31 degrees in our home and almost below zero outside. My son was only three months, and chile he did better than us. We wrapped each other in tons of clothes, put at least 5 pairs of socks on each other's hands. We had our own big quilt covers that we laid in our big bed as a family until sunrise.

The road was covered in black ice, the car wouldn't start, we heard sirens, and people were runnin' around in a panic to neighbor's homes for things they needed. Family back home was calling to see if we wanted a plane ticket back home or if we needed cash for food. They sent what they could. Thankfully, after a long four and a half days of freezin' cold, no power, and barely any mobility people were back outside barbequing and drinking beers like nothin' tragic didn't just happen.

The aftermath led us to public resources and things started rollin' again.

During 2021, I finished up community college then I continued my education at a university. I found another job servicing inmates at the downtown jail. I continued searching for new hobbies and adventures with my family even when things weren't so great.

By 2024? I wasn't just standin.'

I was *movin' different.*

I studied YouTube videos like it was Harvard.

I saved TikTok's like gospel.

I watched reels with a notebook in my lap, takin' notes on brandin,' marketin,' printin,' and pricin.'

Modest Royalteez is goin' to be a BIG-name brand one day!

I saved every dime I could to invest in *me* because nobody else was gonna do it for me.

And maybe you're wonderin,' *why now? Why not before?*

Let me be clear, I wasn't waitin.' I was *preparin.'*

I've checked off goals people said I'd never reach. I've trusted what God whispered into my spirit.

No turnin' back. No shrinkin.' No apologies.

And when I make it?

I'm not just clapping for myself.

I'm bringin' chairs for other women.

I'm buildin' tables where we all eat.

I'm reachin' back through the flames to pull the next one up.

I've worked dead-end jobs that drained my soul and barely paid my bills.

I've smiled at customers while fightin' battles in my spirit.

I've folded clothes for corporations that didn't know my name.

I've clocked in sick, cried durin' lunch breaks, and left jobs with nothin' but hope in my pockets.

But even then, I knew, this ain't it. This can't be it.

Because I wasn't built for survival.

I was born for *purpose*.

To lead.

To love.

To liberate.

Yeah, I'm gettin' a degree. But that ain't my dream. That's just my *net*.

The real dream? The Imaginary Center is a space I've carried in my heart for years.

A sanctuary for kids, teens, and young adults who need more than a classroom.

They need *safety*. They need *guidance*. They need someone who *gets it*.

They need what I needed.

And I'm gonna build it. Not someday.

Soon.

Because I've always been *that person*.

The one folks come to when life breaks them.

The one who listens, holds space, helps them see light in the dark.

Communication? That's my gift.

Not to impress but to *impact*.

But let me be real with you:

I'm not preachin' from some perfect place.

I'm not some Instagram expert pretendin' the journey was smooth.

I've been through it.

Through abuse.

Abandonment.

Betrayal.

Addiction in others and in myself.

I've had days I didn't want to wake up.

Nights I cried so hard my chest went numb.

I've sat in silence, screamin' inside.

I've been overlooked, underestimated, and pushed to the edge.

But I *never gave up*.

Faith and strength aren't just tattoos on my thighs.

They're my *survival kit*.

They remind me that I made it through storms most people don't even talk about.

That even with everythin' stacked against me…

I'm still here.

I didn't just survive. I evolved.

Growing up, I didn't even like the name Amber.

It felt… plain.

Basic.

Not "Black enough."

The girls around me had names that bounced off their tongues: Sha'Nique. Eisha. Unique.

And me? Amber.

I used to feel like I stuck out in the wrong way.

Like I had to *prove* I belonged in my own skin.

I had to be tough; I was comin' up in a rough area. Swag had to be on point and don't show no signs of weakness or people was gone be on yo ass.

I held my own. I was respected by many and hated in the same sense, but one thing about me, I always showed up as myself.

But names carry meaning.

And as I grew, I discovered mine did too.

Amber is *healing*.

It's *warmth*.

It's *protection*.

It's a gemstone that traps light inside it, keeps it safe for centuries.

Funny how they tried to rename me before I even knew myself—fast, angry, too loud, too hard. But they never asked why.

And now?

I wear that name like armor.

Amber is power.

Amber is purpose.

Amber is *me*.

I didn't become this woman overnight.

I was chiseled by chaos.

Polished by pain.

Strengthened by struggle.

And now I shine.

Not because life was easy, but because I chose to shine anyway.

So, if you're readin' this and feelin' broken, tired, invisible—*hold on*.

Your story isn't over.

You can start late.

You can start broke.

You can start scared.

Just start.

Because I'm livin' proof that you can build something beautiful from absolutely *nothing*.

The Girl in the Mirror

There's a girl in the mirror.
She look like me but she don't always feel like me.
Some days I stare, other days I glance quickly and keep it pushin.'
Depends on the day, really. Depends on the mood.

Her face tells stories.
Tired eyes, full lips, brows that don't lie.
You can see the stress, but you can also see the strength.

She got hips.
Thick thighs.
A little belly she is still learnin' to love.
Still workin' on the weight, still dealin' with those little thoughts that creep in:
"You need to tighten up..."
"Damn, you used to be smaller..."
But who don't got somethin' they working through?

Don't get it twisted, I'm not broken.
Just healin' in layers.

Growing up, that mirror used to feel like a test.
I'd stare and pick myself apart, wonderin' if I was good enough.
Hair too short.
Head too wide.
Skin too dark some days, not "Black enough" others.
Name too plain.
Body too muscular for my age.

I used to wish I could trade myself in for somebody else.
Somebody lighter, softer, quieter.

Somebody mamas stayed for.
Somebody daddies showed up for.
Somebody who didn't cry so much behind closed doors.

But I'm not her.
And now?
I don't wanna be.

That girl in the mirror?
She has been through it.
She's made it through things people don't even speak on.

She's still here.
Still learnin.'
Still laughin.'
Still lovin' people.
Still lovin' herself even when it's hard.

I still got my days.
Days I don't feel pretty.
Days I scroll and compare.
Days I try on five outfits before I walk out the house.
But I still walk out. Chin up. Waist not snatched, but confidence loud.

Because I know who I am now.
And even if I don't got it all together, I *got me*.

I don't need to be perfect.
I just need to be *real*.

And that girl in the mirror?
She's real as hell.
She don't fake it for nobody.

Fail to See

She don't shrink no more.
She don't beg for love or settle for silence.

She's finally seein' herself.
Flaws, flyness, and all.

And today?

She still got work to do, but she loves herself enough to keep doin' it.

CHAPTER TWO

THE EARLY YEARS

Oakland roots, childhood truths, and growing up in chaos

Standin' on my own two feet at a young age wasn't easy. Lonely ain't even the word when you ain't got no family to lean on.

I had to carry a load most kids couldn't handle, but that was Thomas' version of discipline.

Call it tough love, call it survival, he always said, "If I don't teach you now, ain't nobody gonna care to teach you later."

Back then, it felt like punishment.

But now? I get it.

Sometimes I do thank him for the way he raised me just not out loud.

Pickin' weeds in the front yard with them raggedy gloves, cleanin' up behind our dog, Jennie, haulin' heavy-ass five-gallon water jugs into the house like I was some kind of pit crew. I didn't need a gym.

That's where these muscles came from.

Truth be told?

I was more of a son to Thomas than a daughter.

I was only seven-years-old.

He used to drag me to his AA meetings. I'd sit there quietly, watchin' grown folks spill their guts about drugs and regrets. I didn't understand it all, but I sat proudly. That was my daddy.

He loved me in his own complicated-ass way. I knew that.

But even as a little girl, I felt the hole he couldn't fill.

There was somethin' missin.'

One day, I found a picture tucked inside an old shoebox with dusty edges curled.

It was me as a baby. In the arms of a woman with beautiful, chinky eyes and a crooked smile.

Michelle. My mother.

Next to her was Thomas— young, slim, still had dreams in his face.

They looked happy.

The kind of love that fades before you even know it's real.

That photo had me in my feelings for days.

Why'd she leave me?

Was I that easy to walk away from?

Did she even cry when she gave me up?

Or did she just float away lighter, leavin' me behind like baggage?

I started hearin' whispers that I had a sister older than me. That Michelle might still be around.

Then my granny, her mama, popped up outta nowhere with photos, letters, and a plan.

She said she was takin' me to visit my mama at Folsom State Prison.

I was just four-years-old the first time I saw Michelle in person.

Thick glass between us. I sat there small, confused, lookin' up at a woman who looked just like me.

I didn't understand how to feel. Was I supposed to cry? Hug the glass? Smile?

I just sat there. Staring.

When she got out, I was ten.

She showed up lookin' like she stepped out of a music video. Long black hair, coke-bottle figure, lollipop in her mouth.

"Hey, baby... I'm your mom."

I just nodded. My stepmom had just did my hair and got me dressed.

Michelle took me out that day. Said she was gonna be involved in my life now.

Said she'd never leave me again.

She gave me some sneakers, size 6. My big feet was bustin' out them lil shoes, but she smiled and said, "I bought these just for you."

I knew she was lyin.' They were hers. But I smiled and accepted them anyway.

She fed me lies wrapped in promises, dressed them up pretty.

And I ate them because I wanted to believe.

Wanted so bad to believe the woman who gave me life could learn to love me, too.

But when she dropped me off at home?

She disappeared again.

Just like the first time.

Michelle wasn't just a troubled woman; she was deep in the streets. She ran with Bloods, got caught up in some mess, and when the heat came down, she snitched. Big white trucks, SWAT, and the Oakland Police Department swarmed the Acorn projects where she and her other kids were livin.' They stormed in like it was a war zone. After that, her name was dirt. Her shiesty ways never stopped, though. Life started showin' on her face. She looked washed up. And in the streets? Once you become a snitch, you can never come back from that. It was crazy growin' up hearin' whispers about my mama.

God says in the Bible, if you take care of your kids, they will take care of you. My mama never did right by hers. She was a covert narcissist, a bully, a liar, deceitful, and connivin.' She never took accountability. And life? Life ain't never good to you when you forsake your children.

After that day, her shiesty ways never stopped. The more dirt she did, the more life started eatin' away at her appearance. She went from fine and full of life to lookin' washed up, tired, and hollow. She never tried to fix herself. Instead, she doubled down on the same mess, makin' her relationships with her children even worse.

I thought we were bondin' when we'd be on the phone gossipin,' me laughin' at her stories and trying so hard to prove I was the daughter she'd been missin' all these years. I wanted her to see me, to love me, to claim me. But her intentions were never to really be my mother. I was just a convenient someone to fill the space until she got tired of me. And when she did, she'd switch me out for one of my other sisters like we were interchangeable.

That was Michelle's way.

She was like warm wind one second, then gone.

No goodbye. Just silence and questions.

Your mother is supposed to be your first friend and teacher but that wasn't my life. She played on my mental and emotions a lot. A girl needs their mother to show them the way of life. Teach them how to be a girl and one day teach them how to become a woman. I didn't get that fate!

I didn't get those girl talks, those teenage prep talks about boys, girls, hygiene, hair, and all the other things that havin' a mom came with. Instead, I got pictures, hearsay, and lies.

Sometimes I'd see her again if my granny picked me up and brought me around.

She always had some man in the house. Random girls she called her "nieces."

Dudes she swore were just "friends" or "homeboys."

The house always had weird energy.

Always some drama.

She'd sit me down, look me in the eye, and lie with a straight face.

"I'm gonna get my life together. Get all my kids back. I'ma be a good mama this time."

But every time I saw her, she looked worse.

More tired. More wild. More gone.

And I finally realized...

She was never gon' be a mama to me.

She knew that the day she gave me up. Deja came into my life with her children Chanel, Rainy, Bianca, and Ronnie and for a long time, they were my everyday reality. My daddy and Deja were together for years, long enough to feel permanent, long enough for love to turn into something ugly. At first, they were in love, but then it got toxic. My daddy had anger in him, mental abuse wrapped up in mood swings, and he couldn't keep his shit in his pants, which stressed Deja out heavy. Still, she tried to be a stepmother the only way she knew how. Me and my step-siblings sometimes we clicked, sometimes we clashed. Rainy was the oldest, mean as hell, conniving, deceitful, and always got away with everything. She ran shit. Whatever she said, we did, or she was gonna whoop our ass. That was big sis. As wild as it sounds, I love her deeply, and as we got older, our relationship healed into something better. Bianca stayed distant, like she never really wanted to be where she was. I still got love for her, even if we don't truly have a relationship. Ronnie left The Nest early. Him and my daddy didn't get along, so he moved out before the girls did, but he was always the brother who checked in, kept me in the loop, and made sure I knew what was going on. I'll always love and respect him for that. Gonna whoop our ass. That was big sis. As wild as it sounds, I love her deeply, and as we got older, our relationship healed into something better.

Me and Chanel though-we were thick as thieves. Fought together, walked together, got in trouble together. That was my baby, always has been, always will be. We also got our asses whooped together, military style. My daddy's discipline depended on his mood one minute we laughing, out having fun, the next minute we lined up getting our asses tore up because of his bipolar ways. If we didn't clean up, he'd wake us up out our motherfucking sleep, either hollering or swinging a belt. When my daddy and Deja finally broke up, my step-siblings moved away, and just like that, the bond got fractured. Years went by with no contact, then it was in and out, in and out-talking here and there, bickering, tension always lingering. It's hard when you go from living on top of each other to feeling like strangers. Still, my daddy talks to Deja and her kids to this day and loves them to death.

And so do I. Blood or not, they were my family-and there's nothing I wouldn't do for them.But let me be real, my childhood wasn't *all* bad.I loved g'tting' gifts from my daddy. Even if he couldn't be consistent, when he came through, he came through. I remember them little surprises like gold, especially when he pulled up with somethin' I ain't even ask for. That shit made me feel seen.

And when we linked up with family who lived hella miles away? Man, those were some of the best times. Road trips, beach days, cookout moments where life felt simple, where everybody laughed like they didn't have problems waitin' for them back home.

I loved sittin' on the meter box with my friends, choppin' it up like we had all the time in the world. No phones. No fake vibes. Just us—posted up, crackin' jokes, talkin' shit, dreamin' about what we'd be one day.

We used to walk in packs around the westside, talkin' loud, laughin' louder, slap boxin' just for fun, darin' each other to do dumb shit. Them *chirp* days? Man, if you know, you know. That Boost chirp was everythin.' We stayed posted with walkies like we was in some spy movie.

My daddy wasn't around for most things after I hit about twelve. Thomas went to prison for beating the shit out of some drug addict faggot that turned his father's house into a trap house. He was always the nigga that had to regulate shit.

Things led to another when he tried to put Henry and our gay cousin out; things got heated and went left quickly. Henry ended up going to the feds and they put a warrant out for his arrest. Thomas missed school events and we didn't have too many heart-to-hearts.

But I'll give him this, he made sure the bills got paid. And my granny? She kept that roof over our heads like her life depended on it. That house held us together when everything else was fallin' apart.

When Thomas went away, it really messed up my mind because that was the only parent I had around and even with the tough love I received, I was grateful that he was present. You feel like you lose half of your heart when you lose a parent. Most days, I sit and think about some things I really admired about Thomas.

When my daddy and Granny cooked? Whew. That food hit *different*. Seasoned with soul, struggle, and love. Even when life felt unstable, that food was solid; it held me.

And honestly? I was naturally funny. I been a clown since a kid. Not goofy, but funny for real. The type of funny that made people forget their pain for a second. The type that kept people wantin' to be around me. I had jokes, and I had *heart*. I was a protector. always lookin' out for the ones around me even when nobody looked out for me.

And nothin' will ever compare to the 90s. That was an *era*.

The best music—SWV, Mary, Tupac, 112.

The best TV—*Moesha, Martin, Living Single, Cousin Skeeter*.

The best games—jump rope, freeze tag, Nintendo, block parties.

The best *love*. Real love. Hood love. Family love.

You had to *be there* to understand.

Yeah, there was hella pain.

But there was magic, too.

And I hold onto that magic like a lifeline.

Back home, life moved on. Thomas had big plans for me.

He was convinced I'd be a basketball star.

Came to all my games, yellin' from the stands like he was coachin.'

"That's my baby! That's mine!"

But I was playin' for him, not me.

The girls on my team weren't nice. They talked slick.

"You look like a boy."

"You dribble like one, too."

I remember this one game when I finally hit a clean three-pointer. I was proud... until I realized I scored on the wrong goal.

The whole gym went silent. Then the laughter hit like bricks.

Thomas laughed, too, tried to play it off.

But that shit broke me.

I never picked up a ball again.

That dream went right into the box where I kept Michelle's promises.

Right next to my tears.

But everythin' changed when I started Bernard Academy.

That school was right across from the projects.

You had to have thick skin and quick hands. It wasn't just about passin' classes; it was about survivin' the day.

On the first day, I walked up and instantly saw how different it was.

Loud girls yellin,' kids fightin,' boys showin' out.

I ain't scare easy, but I felt that pressure.

As I was walkin' to school, I saw this girl walkin' by herself. She was light-skinned, cute, had that "everybody know me" energy. I smiled and said, "Hey, I'm Amber."

She smiled back.

"I'm Rachelle."

We clicked instantly.

She told me she was in sixth grade too, goin' to Bernard, so we walked together. She already had people wavin' at her from cars, shoutin' her name from across the street.

Me? I was just happy to have somebody to walk with.

We found out we had the same classes—english, science, PE. Sat next to each other. Ate lunch together. Shared snacks and notes.

But let me tell you, that school?

Full of drama.

Especially in the cafeteria.

One day, I was standin' there with my tray, and I felt somethin' hit me in the back.

Food. Some sauce covered nuggets.

I turned around and there they go.

The Grow sisters and their loud-ass crew, posted up, laughin.' One girl kept talkin' crazy, throwin' stuff, tryna clown.

I tried to ignore it.

Then one of them walked up and pushed my head back.

I don't even remember blinkin.'

I saw red.

I blacked the fuck out.

Swung on her so hard she stumbled, damn near fell over herself.

I grabbed her, threw her ass down the hill outside the cafeteria– yes, down the hill.

She screamed the whole way down.

Her sister thought she was slick and ran up.

I turned and punched her straight in the face; blood spilled from her nose like a faucet.

Everybody started yellin.' Kids scatterin.' Teachers runnin.'

And Rachelle?

She stood there.

Didn't move.

Didn't say nothin.'

She didn't help me. Didn't jump in.

She just stood there while the other girls held her back.

Later, when we linked up, I looked at her sideways.

"I wouldn't have done you like that."

I ain't press her.

But I didn't forget.

That day taught me somethin' real: not everybody who laughs with you gon' swing with you.

And that was when I started watchin' people different.

Especially girls like Rachelle. Pretty. Popular. But shaky when it was time to ride.

That fight might've gotten me suspended, but it taught me a whole lot more than school ever could.

It taught me how fast people will flip. How girls you walk with in the mornin' will watch you get jumped in the afternoon and not move a muscle. It taught me how to depend on myself because even when I was g'tting' hit from all sides—physically, emotionally, spiritually—I was still standin.'

I ain't fold. I ain't run.

I handled mine.

Yeah, I was only in the sixth grade, but I had already been through more than some grown women. I didn't have a mama showin' up for me. My daddy loved me, sure, but only the way he knew how— rough and distant. I had no blueprint. No soft place to land. Just grit. Just survival. Just me.

That school? Them girls? That fight?

It was just a warm-up for the kind of battles I was gonna face later.

But even then, I knew one thing for sure: I wasn't built like the rest of them.

And I damn sure wasn't cut from the same cloth.

Most people thought I was just some angry little Black girl with a deep voice and a bad attitude. They ain't know the half of it.

I didn't hang with a crowd. It was mostly just Rachelle and a couple others. I had associates, people I'd say wassup to in the hallways, maybe crack a joke with at lunch but that was it. I stayed in my own bubble. Partly 'cause I didn't trust nobody, and partly 'cause I learned the more people around you, the more drama comes with 'em.

Still, even in my little bubble, folks stayed in my business. Teasin' me for everything— my big forehead, my voice, my walk, the way I dressed. "She sound like a man," they'd say. "She look hard." I'd walk past groups of kids and hear them giggle or whisper, but I kept my head up. I had to.

Some of them boys that teased me was the same ones who wanted to be in my face later, tryna holler.

That part always tripped me out. I wasn't out here sleepin' around like the rest of the girls in my age group. They were already gettin' bussed down at twelve and fourteen! They clowned or chased boys. I was probably one of the few girls in the school who wasn't havin' sex. Still, somehow I was the one being judged. I got labeled fast and grown, not because of what I was doing, but because of how I carried myself. Strong. Loud. Not backin' down. That scared people, especially when it came in form of a little girl.

I used to fight. A lot. Came to school angry most days. The kind of angry that don't even have words just shows up in how hard you walk, how quick you snap, how you keep your hands balled up in fists even when you try to chill.

Sometimes I was the class clown. Sometimes I was the one disruptin' the whole lesson. But even with all that I was smart. Smart-smart.

I won awards that kids twice my age wasn't touchin.' Best Writing Award in the whole city of Oakland. That wasn't no small thing. I was just a sixth grader with a big forehead, crooked glasses, and a lot of hurt but I was still out-writin' older kids. I won the Great American Race Award, A-B honor roll, even made straight A's one semester. That wasn't luck. That was me puttin' my pain on paper, turnin' it into somethin' they had to clap for.

I stayed out the mix for a reason, though. That time in Oakland? It was heavy. Everybody was tryna prove themselves either with fists, a crew, or a gun. Gangs were deep. Cliques were everywhere. The streets didn't wait for you to grow up; they tried to eat you alive.

And truth be told, the adults failed me long before the streets did.

My daddy had two-women syndrome. Always bouncin' from one broken woman to the next. And them women? Most of them were mean as hell to me. Violent, bitter, and jealous like they saw me as a threat instead of a little girl. Some of 'em put their hands on me. There was stuff he ain't even know 'cause I was too scared or too ashamed to say it.

My grandma's friend used to beat on me, too. Her daughter once cut my hair off. They'd stuff me in closets, lock the door, let me scream until I passed out. And the way they looked at me? Like I was dirty. Like I didn't belong. Like just breathin' around them was too much.

There was one time... I don't think I talked about it in the book yet. If I did, forgive me. But if I didn't yeah, I was kidnapped once.

One of my daddy's ex-girlfriends broke into the house with a couple dudes. Took me. Snatched me up and left me in an abandoned house like I was trash. My daddy had to come get me. That was real-life. Not no movie. That was what it meant to be Amber.

He didn't know how to be a father, not really. He gave me the basics—roof over my head, food, clothes. But even that came with rules I didn't understand. I dressed like a boy half the time. Not 'cause I wanted to, but 'cause that was what they bought for me. He raised me the way he would raise a son—tough, quiet, always watchin.' Taught me to keep my guard up. To stay sucker-free. To think like a hustler. To protect myself at all costs.

And while I get it now that was the only way he knew, I didn't get to be soft. I didn't get too many hugs. I didn't get talks about my personal feelings. I got game. I got silence. I got darkness.

He used to hide out in dark rooms for hours, and eventually I started doin' it, too. Just sittin' in the pitch-black, feelin' like that was the only place I could breathe. That depression? That anger? I inherited it. Not on purpose, but because nobody taught me how to feel safe. Nobody gave me a safe place to feel.

So yeah, I walked into school angry.

But I walked in smart, too.

I remember when my dad would have his happy moments when he would wake up and want to throw a fish fry. Those were some moments that I looked forward to! He would be whistlin' and singin' *Don't Leave Me Girl* by the R&B group Blackstreet. Boy he would be thumpin' his foot, cuttin' up that fresh catfish he caught while my granny was cuttin' up fresh potatoes and makin' salad. Hmm Hmm Hmm, those were the good ol' days.

CHAPTER THREE

THE SHIFT

The moment everything changed
mentally, emotionally, spiritually

B reathing heavily, my face twisted in anger, I glared at everyone starin' at me through the window while I sat in the back of the police car, all the kids outside watchin' in shock.

The officers drove me around to the front of the school; they pulled over, opened my door, and pulled me out of the car.

The handcuffs were on pretty tight like I was some kind of criminal. One of the buff cops opened the door for me and grabbed me by the arm to take me into the principal's office. I sat down in the chair while the cops explained to the administrators what occurred. Here comes Principal Kindal.

"Amber, right?"

"Yea."

"Come with me back to my office." She slammed the door. "So, you had a fight, huh?"

"Yea, that's what it look like?"

"Don't get smart with me. You on your way to juvenile. That girl you beat up is injured pretty badly."

"She came up on me puttin' her hands on me first and she was with a crowd of people harassin' me and throwin' things at me and I'm in trouble?"

"Ms. Crown, violence is not tolerated at all no matter who is right or wrong! Both parties will get consequences."

"Ugh. She deserved it!"

"Ms. Crown, you need to change your attitude. You are in deep water."

"Tuh, I know how to swim." I leaned back in my chair thinkin.'

I was really a class clown, not a forced troublemaker. Always crackin' jokes, roastin' people, makin' the whole classroom laugh even the teacher sometimes. That was my escape. If I could make people laugh, it kept me from cryin.' I actually liked school. I went every day, and stayed on top of things because deep down I wanted more for myself.

But truth be told, I didn't always *want* to be there.

It wasn't the work. It was the way I felt. Like I was one of the most hated girls in school and I never understood why. I didn't do shit to nobody but defend myself. I wasn't scary. I didn't fold under pressure. And that made some people mad. Some girls didn't like me off the strength of my confidence or maybe my energy was too real for them to be fake around.

Still, there were some people I *looked forward* to seein.' The ones who were cool, who didn't bring drama, who liked to joke and be goofy like me. They made it bearable. That was what kept me walkin' through those school doors every day, even when I felt like the walls hated me.

"Well, Amber, it is out of my hands. I have to write an incident report. The law is taking it into their own hands. I have to call your guardian."

"Ughh, I'm gon' to get in trouble." Tears started rollin' down my face.

Principal Kindal picked up the phone and dialed my home phone.

Ring, Ring, Ring.

"Hello." I heard my granny clear as day.

"Hello, ma'am, how are you doing this morning?"

"What's wrong? Is everything ok with my granddaughter?"

"No, ma'am. I hate to be the bearer of bad news, but Amber is in my office in handcuffs."

"Oh God I'm on my way."

"What is your name?"

"I'm Ms. Crown."

"Ok, Ms. Crown, there are two officers here and they want to take Amber to juvenile because the other young lady that was involved in the fight was injured pretty badly, and it is out of my hands. The school board is not pleased with this, and they want to take Amber out of the school district and place her in opportunity school."

My granny was angry and in tears.

"I'm on my way." Then all I heard was the dial tone.

"Amber, your granny is on her way, and we are going to sit here and wait for her to arrive because you are a minor."

I slid down the chair with tears comin' from my eyes and my lips poked out. Ten minutes went by, and I heard my granny. "Where is the front office? I'm looking for my baby. I need to know where she is."

I got up and yelled, "Granny, I'm over here." She rushed over to me and hugged me.

"oh my God, baby, are you alright?"

"Yes I am. Did you tell my dad?"

"Yea, I did?"

"What did he say?"

"He said he knew it was going to happen. He seen the crowd when he dropped you off in the parking lot and they looked like they were following you."

"Well, they were, Granny, and now I'm gonin' to juvie." My granny turned to the officers.

"Please don't take her, please.

"Ma'am, we have to. You are more than welcome to come down there and get things figured out, but she was fighting and harmed that girl."

"She is in the 8th grade I am only in the 6th grade. She is older and taller than me and you guys are punishin' me for defendin' myself."

Granny yelled, "BULLSHIT! You guys are full of shit. My baby is so young, and she was attacked."

"As we stated, ma'am, you can come down to the juvenile detention center on 1752 Greg Rd."

"Amber, I'm going to be right behind y'all. Ok, Pooh Bear. I got you. I'm going to call your dad."

"Ok, Mama."

The officers grabbed me by the arm and walked me to the car. When we finally got to juvenile hall, they sat me down in a room. "You're going to have someone come after we go get your grandmother and they will talk to you both about the next steps."

The door slammed and I slammed my head down on the desk.

"How did I get here? What's gon' to happen to me? Man, this is so crazy. I just know when it's all over, I'm gon' to get a whooping and a harsh punishment. My dad don't play."

My granny finally came into the room. She was hysterical.

"Man, Amber, what did I tell you? Don't get into any trouble because look what's going on we here."

"Ok, blame me. It's all my fault. People been pickin' on me for two days and a crowd of people I don't know against me. I hate myself."

My granny looked at me with an evil face, she wasn't tryna hear nothin' I had to say.

You know old people, you couldn't tell them nothin.' They believed what they wanted to believe. I knew I had a temper, but I wasn't at-fault and after all, my daddy told me if somebody got in the fire range to fire off on they ass.

The door opened and it was a youth development officer with a clipboard and some papers. She greeted us and took a seat.

"Hey, Amber, how are you feeling?"

"Horrible."

"Well, I am sorry we are meeting on these circumstances, and I got the incident report from school, and I want to help you."

"You are gone to help my baby!"

"Yes, ma'am, because this is her first offense and she was attacked."

"That's right, they can't fault my baby because she can fight."

"Well, Ms. Crown, I agree she was defending herself and I don't think Amber is a bad child, she just got into a bad situation."

"So where are you going to issue her a citation and give her community service. Thank God so she's not actually going to jail."

"No, Ms. Crown, she is not going to stay here, just fill out these papers."

"Amber, make sure you follow the rules and find community service and do your hours, so you don't get into any more trouble because you don't want to end up back here."

"Thank you so much. Can you get them to take these cuffs off me please."

"Yes, hold on." She slid the chair back and got up to go get one of the officers to take off the handcuffs.

"Alright, Amber and Ms. Crown, y'all are free to go."

"Thank you so much for helping my baby."

"No problem." We walked out and headed to the parking lot.

"Mama."

"Yes, Pooh."

"I know my dad is going to be mad, ain't he?"

"You know your dad, Amber. Ain't no telling with him. Just don't give him no attitude and just go in speak and then go to your room."

We finally made it home and the house was quiet as a mouse, not a radio or TV was playin.'

I walked into my bedroom and plopped on my bed, heart racing and sweatin' bullets not knowin' what was coming next. Footsteps came up the hallway, and I finally heard the door crack open.

"Amber, come here."

"Oook."

I raised up from my bed and followed behind my dad into his room. He sat on the sofa couch that he had in his room, and he said, "What's going on?"

"Well, Dad, I got into a fight today at school."

"Was it those girls I seen in the big crowd?"

"YES!"

"I knew it." He laughed.

"Well, if you knew, why did you leave me at school if you felt those girls were after me?"

"Well," he coughed. "Baby, I didn't think it would go down that way but shit you my child. I already knew you was going to get down."

"I had no choice, Dad. They would not stop followin' me and callin' me names and throwin' things at me. Then she hit me, and I snapped."

"Yea, I hope you did whoop her ass. You know what I told you when somebody get in fire range light they ass up." He chuckled. "Gone and get you a trash bag and some gloves and go pull them weeds and pick up the trash. Oh, and don't forget to take your dog for a walk."

It was 113 degrees outside. My eyes rolled into the back of my head. I was not in the mood to do yardwork and walk the dog in extreme heat. It beat gettin a whoopin' for sure. I went to the kitchen to find some gloves and to get a trash bag. I grabbed my visor out of the room and headed outside to the front yard.

The sun was coming down so hard on my arms, sweat dripped down my face and under my shirt. It was so many weeds down in the ground and he would make me come out here in this heat. I guess this was my punishment. I didn't even know why I was doin' this anyway. I just beat this girl up and he actin' like he wasn't proud. An hour go by, and I heard the front door gate open.

"You almost through?"

"Yes, Dad, I just have to do the ones by the rose bush, and I will be finished."

He went and got the dog and tied her leash to the water hose then went in the house to get Jeannie's water bowl. Thirty minutes went by, and I finally finished the yard. I went to wash my hands really good. "Come on, Jeannie, let's go for a walk."

Pacin' down the street, Jeannie barked at all the cars and the kids we walked past. "Stop, girl. You scarin' the kids." She began breathin' hard and slowin' down.

She walked over to the tree and used the bathroom. Jeannie was goin' to walk about more street and I was turnin' around; it was hot. We started walkin' down International Blvd and I saw a couple of people from school, and they started callin' my name.

"Girl! You beat the hell out of that girl!"

"You sure did. You gave her ass a two four piece and a biscuit and then threw her down the hill."

"I thought she was dead, man."

"Well, you fuck around and find out, huh." We all started laughin.'

"When will you come back to school?"

"I'm not sure. I have to ask my granny how long they got me out of school."

"Okay, well I hope to see you soon."

"Okay bet! I gotta get home and put this dog in the house. I'll see y'all soon." We parted ways. Me and Jeannie ran back to the house.

"Am-berrr."

"Yes, Ma?"

"You hungry?"

"Yes! I'm starvin.'"

"Ok, Pooh. I'm making some tacos."

"Ouuuuuuuuu MY FAVORITE!"

"You know Mama gone hook it up for you."

"C'mon, Jeannie, in the backyard. Outside, outside." Her feet began to pace quickly to the backyard.

"Ma, I'm gon' to go use the bathroom and freshen up before I eat."

"Ok, Pooh Bear."

As I was comin' out the bathroom, my dad said, "I'm going fishing with your uncle. I'll be home later, make sure you clean, and you know it ain't no outside, right?"

"Yes, I know."

"Amber, your plate is on the table." My granny knew I wanted about five or six tacos. Boy, was I greedy. Her famous tacos were so good; I mean bomb! I loved when the orange juices came runnin' down my hand, that was how I knew the tacos were gon' to be fire! Granny got everybody in the neighborhood making tacos and toppin' it with pepper and ketchup.

"Ma, I'm about to go shower. I'm full."

"Ok, baby, I love you."

"I love you, too."

Headin' down the hallway, I turned on the light and grabbed some towels. I twisted the shower nob to steamin' hot, that was how I liked my showers. The steam began to fill the bathroom quickly. I leaned my head with my hand over the back of my neck. I exhaled and tears began to fall down my face thinkin' about my father's disappointment in me. I could never seem to get through to him. He wasn't much of a talker and he was an emotionless person. I didn't know if Thomas cared about me or if he didn't know how to care, most days he drank himself to sleep in his dark room.

Most days he wouldn't even speak to me because he was so buried in darkness. So many thoughts raced through my head. I wondered if I was gon' to get beaten when he came back home from gettin' suspended from school. You never knew with him. I just knew I had to stay out of his way. I washed up and got out of the shower and went to my room to get dressed.

Since I was on punishment, all I could do was stare at the TV or sleep. I just turned over and buried my face in my pillow until I fell asleep.

Hours had passed by and I had one eye open and the other one closed shut, starin' at my clock. It was 9:30 pm.

I got up to use the bathroom.

I remember standin' in the bathroom, just starin' at myself in the mirror like I was lookin' at a stranger. My eyes looked hollow, my skin looked different. I didn't even feel real. It was like I had floated out of my body and was watchin' some other girl stand there still, empty, violated.

I didn't cry. I couldn't. I just felt...numb. Like somethin' got snatched outta me that I would never get back.

I wanted to scream, but I couldn't even speak. My throat felt tight like if I opened my mouth, the world would swallow me whole. I was scared. Scared of my daddy. I was scared he was gon' to beat me to death.

After the fight, I moved around the house on eggshells because I knew shit wasn't sweet and even though I won, my dad would contradict himself as long as he was right to him and I played like I understood I was good.

I just kept thinkin' to myself. I didn't wanna be another girl who folks whispered about. I didn't wanna be the one they looked at sideways in class or called fast behind my back. I didn't wanna lose my label as a "good girl," even if that label had already been ripped away from me without my permission.

So, I stood there. Quiet. Frozen. Filthy.

Before I could get up good, I heard another knock at the door.

"Amber."

"Yes, Dad?"

"Come to my room."

"I wanted to talk to you about what happened at school the other day and why you're on punishment."

"Yes, Dad."

"Tell me what happened again. How did you end up fighting ol' girl?"

"Dad, I told you she kept botherin' me, her and her friends and they were followin' me. Throwin' things at me and she was pushin' my head, and I had to beat her up."

"Hahahahaha!" my dad laughed loudly. I began to laugh and suddenly my dad stopped laughin.' "Why didn't you walk away, Amber?"

"I tried, Dad."

"How come you didn't look for a fuckin' teacher! A police officer, a hall monitor, some fuckin' body, Amber!"

I started gettin' hot and I felt like I was startin' to catch a fever. My eyes began to fill up with tears because I was confused why my dad was mad at me for defending myself and he told me he wasn't raisin' any punks.

I did the very thing he always preached to me about and he was mad at me. He began to get up and go to his closet to reach for his long, thick black belt. He shut the closet and walked past me.

"You can't be getting kicked out of school and…"

"But, Dad, she hit me first."

He told me I should have been thinkin' about gettin' in trouble for gettin' kicked out of school then he told me to turn around, and I burst out in tears.

"I bet you will learn to listen after this ass whoopin.'"

I watched his hand, and the belt go way up in the air and come down fast and before I knew it, he was tearin' my ass up.

I got hit at least twenty times and I even fell on the ground tryna block the rest of the hits with my hands. It seemed like the more I did that, the harder he hit me. The belt popped me in the face three times.

"GET YO ASS UP, NIGGA! Now you go lay yo ass down before I give you something else to cry about."

I quickly got up and ran to my room, screamin' and cryin.' My legs were so bruised, red, and whelped. Snot came runnin' down my nose and my legs felt numb. I had the most detest feelin' toward my dad in that very moment. I was tired of his bi-polar ways and the contradiction. He was no different than these niggas that be out here lyin.'

I couldn't wait to go back to school. I couldn't stand to be in this house.

The next morning, my granny knocked on the door and told me everythin' was gon' to be ok and that she loved me. She kissed me on my forehead and hugged me tightly.

"Now, come on, Amber. We to have a meeting with the principal and the school dean about deciding to let you back in school."

"Okay, Granny. I'm gettin' dressed now."

I went to my closet to look for a black blouse and black slacks. I bent down, and I grabbed my church shoes. I had to make it look like I wanted to be back in school since they called me a menace.

After I got done gettin' dressed, I went to meet my granny outside at the car. She was takin' a little smoke break. She loved her Cool One Hundreds.

I said, "Granny, when you gonna stop smokin'?"

"Amber, when I die." We both laughed.

My granny put her cigarette out and we hopped in the car on our way to Bernard Academy. When my granny parked, she said, "Amber, don't go in this meeting talking back. Fix your face, don't frown, and just listen to what these people got to say, OK!"

"Yes, Ma, but you do know it wasn't my fault to begin with."

"Amberrrrr!"

"Okay, Ma. Okay, Ma. I'm gonna be on my best behavior."

"Thank you, Pooh. That's what I wanna hear."

As we walked through the halls, the other students stared at me, and I heard whispers.

"There go Amber. She whooped that girl ass." Then they all began to laugh.

"Yeah, she threw that girl right down the hill, that's what she get though. You know she kept picking on Amber and Amber did what she had to do."

I had a smirk on my face; I felt like I was that girl. I beat up somebody way older than me and it was crucial to the whole school; they started to look up to me. I knew that I was gon' to be that beast. I knew I was that bully; I bullied the bullies! My granny opened the door to the principal's office and the principal walked up to us.

"Hello, Ms. Crown. I hope you're doing better than the last time that I saw you."

She spoke in the nastiest tone tryna be nice.

It was a bittersweet moment. She was so fake; I knew she didn't want me here to begin with but that was ok. I was gonna give them what they wanted, and I was gonna do what my granny wanted me to do because she always wanted what was best for me.

"Let's have a seat and discuss the plan for Amber. I've decided we will give Amber another chance here, but under no circumstances can she get into any more trouble, or she will be sent to opportunity school."

"Yes, Principal Kindal, she understands. I had a long talk with her, and she will not be getting in anymore trouble. I will make sure of it."

"Amber, you understand how serious we are. We want you to be your best and even with your academics. Your grandmother is a sweet lady, and she loves you and is putting her neck out to make sure you get your education."

"I understand, Principal Kindal. I'll stay out of trouble. Thank you for lettin' me come back to school, I won't disappoint you."

"You're free to come back after the summer, Amber. We will see you then."

Me and my granny slowly got up and she smiled at me and told me she loved me. My granny was always so warm with me and stood behind me no matter what! I was the daughter she never had. I pushed my chair in and followed behind my granny to the parking lot.

As we pulled out the school's parking lot, I saw the girl Brielle, her sister, and mom gettin' out the car, walkin' into the school. My face immediately hardened! I tensed up and I was ready to roll my window down and talk big shit to ol' girl and her family.

I just stared until they vanished. My granny turned on the music. Tina Marie's *Square Bizness* was playin.' That was our jam. I started singin' and clappin'; it was always a vibe without Thomas.

He always seemed like there was a chip on his shoulder unless it was about him and what he wanted to do. Life was sweet when I wasn't around him. We ended up stoppin' at Church's Chicken.

"How may I take your order?"

"Yes, can I get a 12-piece family meal with mashed potatoes and gravy, French fries, and two corn on a cob."

"What sauce?"

"Extra salt, butter, and honey, please."

"What would you like for your drinks?"

"One Pepsi and one Sprite."

"Will that be all for you?"

"Yes"

"$23.99. To the first window, please pull forward."

"Ouweeee, I cannot wait to eat."

My granny paid for the food and got our bag and drinks before pullin' off.

"You think my dad is going to be happy that I'm back in school?"

"Amber, don't worry about it. He will be just fine."

We pulled into the driveway, and my dad was outside waterin' the rose bush. I slowly got out the car and my granny spoke first.

"Hey, son."

"Hey, Mama."

"Hi, Dad."

"Hey, baby, everything alright?"

"Yes, I can go back to school." He smiled.

"That's what I'm talking about."

"We got some Church's, Dad, if you want some."

"Alright, just leave mine in the bag and sit mine to the side."

"I got chu."

I tore that food down; my belly was pokin' out. It was time for me to wash up and get ready for school tomorrow... I slowly got up and washed my hands, threw my mess away, and headed to my room to get my things ready so I could take a shower.

The next morning, I walked into school with my head up, fresh fit on, hair laid. But the same girl I fought last week was mad-dogging me from across the hall. I ain't break eye contact. She looked away first.

The whole school was talkin' 'bout me. Folks givin' me high-fives, whisperin' in the halls, actin' like I was a legend or somethin.'

"That's the girl that beat Tasha's ass."

"She top dog now."

But that didn't last long.

Later that week, I got into it again. This time, with a girl from the 60s Crip gang. It popped off in class. She said somethin' slick, and I stood up.

"What you say?"

She stood, too. "You heard me."

Next thing I knew, desks were flyin.' We was on the floor, hair-pullin,' fists swingin.' Security came rushin' in, and I was dragged out the room in cuffs.

This time, they wasn't playin.' I got kicked out the whole district.

When my dad found out, he was heated. Threatened to beat me. I was scared. I knew I had to beat him home. I was walkin' fast; he was drivin' beside me, yellin' out the window. I hit the corner and hopped the fence, took off.

I ended up in the projects to go see Michelle. She was in there with a few Piru Bloods, snortin' coke, playin' dominoes, g'tting' high. When I walked in, she looked at me like she ain't even know me.

"What you doin' here?"

"Michelle... I needed somewhere to go."

"This ain't the place for you. I don't wanna hear 'bout you and your daddy. I bet not hear you out here fuckin' or suckin' either, or I'll drag yo ass on Bloods."

I left. Never went home.

Later, I met up with Keisha, a hood rat from school.

"I ran away. My dad was about to beat my ass for g'tting' kicked out again."

"Girl, same. My mama threw me out. Told me to get out her face."

"I don't have nowhere to go."

"Come on, girl, I got somewhere."

We walked all over to the westside. I saw a few folks I knew.

We pulled up to Kash's house. Four other dudes were there, smokin,' chillin.' *Lovers and Friends* was playin' low on the radio. Keisha went to the back.

Next thing I knew, I could hear her moanin' loud. Two dudes were runnin' a train on her. I sat in the front room, uncomfortable. Kash started talkin' to me.

"You too pretty to be out here like this. What you doin' messin' with that lame nigga, Johnathan?" He slid closer. "You need a real nigga like me."

"Nah, I love my boyfriend."

He got up, grabbed a Bible. "I put that on God and my mama, on the set, I won't say nothin'."

He started kissin' my neck. I pulled away.

"Stop, Kash." He stood, jumped in front of me.

"C'mon, I got you." He grabbed my arm. I started pullin' back.

"Stop, Kash!"

He dragged me, pushed me into the back room, and locked the door. Then he pulled a gun out and pointed it at my face. I was terrified! Shakin' and prayin' to the Lord above he didn't accidently pull the trigger.

"Get up and shut up."

"Please, Kash, I'm still a virgin."

He laughed. "Damn, Johnathan ain't hit that yet? He such a square."

He put the gun on the dresser, came up on me, and pulled my pants down. When he kissed me down there, tears poured from my eyes.

He shoved his finger up me. "OUCH"! His nails were sharp. It hurt. Bad.

"Take your shirt off. Lay on the bed."

He reached in the drawer for a condom then climbed on top of me.

"Open your legs, bitch."

"Kash, please get off me."

He started grindin' on me. I squeezed my legs shut. I cried out to God.

I prayed…I froze…

He stopped and looked me in my eyes.

"Get out my house. Get your shit and get the fuck out."

I threw my clothes on and ran. Keisha was already outside smokin.'

"Amber, what's wrong?"

I shook my head and wiped my face. We walked in silence. She knew. By the look on my face, somethin' tragic happened to me.

That night, helicopters were flyin' low. Police were all over the neighborhood. Every time I saw a car, I ducked and hid.

One cop car slowed down beside me.

"What's your name?"

"Amber."

"Your dad and grandmother are worried sick. Come with us. We'll get you home."

Before I could say bye, Keisha took off runnin.' She wasn't my friend anyway.

We pulled up to the house. My granny was pacin' the driveway. As soon as she saw me, she ran to the car.

"Amber!"

"Yes, Ma. I'm here." She hugged me so tight then started bawlin.'

"You coulda been killed. I was so worried." Her face fell with disappointment.

We walked inside. My dad was on the couch, head down. Silent.

Two minutes passed.

"You alright, baby?" he finally asked.

"Yes, Dad."

"You hungry?"

"No."

He nodded and walked to his room.

I went to mine, grabbed some night clothes, and took a hot shower. I scrubbed the filth off me. I cried harder than ever before. I felt dirty. I felt like the worst daughter alive.

I got out the shower and looked in the mirror... I felt so gross. Tears filled my eyes, thinkin' to myself how I was gon' to go on like this.

The next morning, my dad was full of questions.

"Where you been? Who were you with? What the hell is wrong with you?"

When I didn't answer fast enough, he snapped.

"You think this is a joke? I done told you! I will beat your ass!"

The phone rang and I was happy for the interruption.

He picked it up, listened quietly, and his demeanor changed. "That was about my father. He's real sick. I gotta go to Arizona," he said then packed and left.

That week with my granny was peaceful. We cooked, watched shows, and she braided my hair. She never asked about Kash. But I knew she knew.

My granny was my mother and even though I didn't tell her about bein' raped, she knew there was somethin' I was not tellin' her.

I talked to God about it; I was angry. I felt defeated. I wanted to tell my granny but I didn't think she would have taken it well. Tellin' Thomas was hella out.

Then Friday night came.

We were sittin' on the porch and heard sirens. My dad's car came flyin' down the street with two cop cars right behind him.

He pulled into the driveway and jumped out.

"GET DOWN! HANDS IN THE AIR!" They tackled him, kicked him, then cuffed him. Me and my granny screamed. I tried to run to him.

"Get your nigger ass back in the house before we shoot you, too!"

"Amber, come on, baby!"

"No! DAD!"

They slammed him into the squad car. His eyes met mine for a split second.

That was the last time I would see my father for years.

And that was the night my life would never be the same again.

CHAPTER FOUR

CYCLES & SURVIVAL

*Breaking patterns, fighting pain,
and learning the hard way*

The morning came slow, like even the sun ain't wanna get up. The light crept through the blinds, weak and tired, spillin' across my room like it didn't have the energy to shine.

Everything felt heavy– my body, my heart, the whole damn house.

From the kitchen, I heard it. Granny's cryin.' Not no soft cry either. This was a deep, gut-pullin' sobs like the kind where pain grabbed your throat and wouldn't let go. It wasn't just a sound; it was *hurt* fillin' the whole house.

I froze with my chest tight, listenin.' Granny was always the strong one, the one holdin' everybody else up. Hearin' her break like that made me want to crawl out of my skin.

I already knew what it was about.

My daddy had just been arrested. They were transportin' him back to Arizona to do real-time.

Not a couple nights in county. Not a slap on the wrist. *Real-time.*

And though part of me didn't want that for him—prison, that kind of pain—I couldn't deny that another part of me felt relief. He was gone.

That sounds cold, but it was real.

There were times when I wanted to run away before but I imagined I ran away and found peace and happiness. A huge village!

My daddy was hard. Never gentle. Always on edge like he was ready to snap at any second. He made sure I had food in my stomach and clothes on my back, but love? Nurturing? That man would tell me he loved me but wouldn't show it physically as a father should.

No askin' how my day went.

No soft moments.

Just rules. Just discipline.

He didn't know how to comfort me, only how to command. And me? I just wanted to *breathe*. To live without feelin' like I was always under a microscope, always one mistake away from punishment.

So yeah, when the cops came and hauled him off, my heart twisted in two directions. Sadness and relief tangled up together like barbed wire.

A couple days later, the house felt even heavier. Granny was sittin' on the edge of the couch in her nightgown, holdin' her Bible tight with both hands like it was the only thing keepin' her together. Her eyes looked tired like she'd been carryin' the weight of the whole world and our family on her back for too long.

"Amber," she said softly, her voice scratchy from cryin.' "I'ma check myself into Kaiser. They gotta run some tests."

My stomach dropped. Granny was my rock, my safe place. The idea of her bein' gone, even just for a couple nights, made my chest hurt.

"I packed a bag already," she continued. "I need you to hold this house down for me. Don't let nobody in here unless it's family and keep things clean. You hear me, baby?"

"Yes, ma'am," I said quickly, tryna sound grown, tryna sound ready, even though I felt anything but.

She gave me one of those long, tight hugs that felt like they'd hold you together when you were about to fall apart. Then she kissed my forehead and whispered, "I'm trustin' you, Amber. Don't make me regret it."

"I won't, Granny."

I stood at the window and watched her car roll slowly down the block until it turned the corner and disappeared.

When she was outta sight, I felt two things at the exact same time:

Sadness, 'cause the house already felt emptier without her... and freedom like I could finally breathe without somebody watchin' my every move.

The first night alone, the silence was so loud; it felt like it was chokin' me.

I laid on my bed, starin' at the ceilin,' thinkin' about *everything*.

Daddy was locked up again, Granny was in the hospital, Mama was nowhere to be found... and me? I was just a young girl tryna survive it all.

My mind kept driftin' back to Kash's house. To that night I'd been tryin' so hard to forget. The things he did to me; the things I never told a soul. It haunted me, sat heavy on my chest like a secret that might kill me if I didn't let it out.

But I couldn't tell anybody.

So, I kept it locked inside, hidin' behind fake smiles and jokes, acting like life was normal when inside I was breakin.'

Music became my medicine.

I'd put my headphones on, close my eyes, and disappear.

Amanda Perez when I was sad. Trina when I was feelin' myself. Tynisha Keli when I needed to feel love. Sammie when I wanted to just drift away. Whatever mood I was in, there was a song for it.

Music understood me when nobody else did.

And when the music wasn't enough, I wrote. My notebook was my best friend, the only one who really knew the truth. I poured my soul onto those pages—pain, anger, love, confusion– all of it.

One entry that week read:

"I'm tired of bein' the strong one. Tired of people thinkin' I got it together just 'cause I don't break down in front of them. I hug folks who wouldn't hold me if I was breakin.' I love people who forget I exist unless they need somethin.' I ain't heartless. I'm just hurt. And I don't know who gon' notice before I disappear."

I read those words over and over until the paper blurred from my tears.

I never let anyone see that side of me. To them, I was the funny one, the fighter, the strong friend. But on those pages, I was just Amber—raw, unfiltered, broken in places nobody could see.

Some nights, I'd sit by the window, lookin' out at the streetlights glowin' like little halos in the dark. I'd imagine another life, one where my family was whole, where I didn't have to fight every single day just to feel like I mattered.

In those daydreams, there was peace. Laughter. Safety.

Sometimes I'd cut out pictures from magazines of houses, clothes, vacations, and taped them to my wall, makin' a vision board of the life I swore I'd have one day.

That was my escape. My promise to myself that this wasn't forever.

The next day, I needed to get out of my own head, so I slid over to Rachelle's block.

As soon as I turned the corner, I saw her, Brielle, and Creshae sittin' on the porch, a bag of Hot Cheetos between them, talkin' loud, and laughin' like always.

As soon as they spotted me, Rachelle jumped up, arms wide. "Ayyy, Amber!"

I couldn't help but smile. For a second, it felt like everything was normal again.

We hugged, and then the jokes started flyin.'

"Girl, you late," Brielle teased, side-eyeing me.

"I had stuff to do," I said, laughin,' playfully swattin' at her.

We fell right into that easy rhythm we'd always had laughin,' clownin,' talkin' about boys, and how crazy seventh grade had been, and how eighth grade was right around the corner.

For those few minutes, I let myself just *be*. No stress, no secrets, no family drama. Just a regular girl chillin' with her friends.

Then Brielle leaned forward, her voice dropped. "For real though, Amber... how's your granny? We heard she been real sick." The laughter died down. I swallowed hard and nodded.

"Yeah," I said softly. "She's at Kaiser right now. They keepin' her for tests."

Their faces shifted immediately, sympathy shinin' in their eyes.

"We love yo' granny," Rachelle said, reachin' out to touch my arm. "She always been sweet to us. We prayin' for her."

"Real talk," Brielle added. "She like the only adult who actually treat us like we matter."

Hearin' that made me feel seen like they understood how much Granny meant to me.

I looked down nervously then said quietly, "My daddy got locked up, too... They sendin' him back to Arizona. He prolly doin' time for a while."

The whole porch went silent.

"Damn," Creshae said first, shakin' her head. "Amber... I'm sorry, girl."

"You good? Like really good?" Rachelle asked, searching my face. I shrugged, fightin' back tears.

"I don't even know. I just... feel numb." They all nodded like they understood.

"It's always us," Brielle muttered. "Black families go through the most."

We sat there in a heavy silence for a moment, the weight of all our pain hangin' in the air.

Even though we were young, none of us were innocent. We'd all been through things kids shouldn't have had to go through.

After a while, the mood lightened again. We laughed, told stories, and made plans for the weekend.

But I noticed Rachelle gettin' quieter as the conversation went on. She wasn't laughin' as much, just watchin' me with this weird look I couldn't quite read.

When it was time to go, we hugged like usual, but something in her vibe felt… off.

Later that evening, one of my classmates pulled me aside at the corner store.

"Yo, Amber," she said, lowerin' her voice. "Rachelle been talkin.' She sayin' you fake, actin' like you better than everybody just 'cause you gettin' all this sympathy. She said you always try to make stuff about you."

My heart dropped.

Rachelle? My Rachelle?

I forced a laugh, tryna play it cool, but it stung.

We'd been through so much together. Why would she say that?

That night, I logged onto MySpace, and sure enough Rachelle had deleted me.

No warnin.' No message. Just *gone*.

I sat there starin' at the screen, hurt and angry all at once.

Finally, I updated my status: **Don't trust nobody.**

And I meant every word.

Around that same time, I started seein' Johnathan more.

He wasn't like Kash.

Where Kash was all control and aggression, Johnathan was soft and patient.

The type to hold my hand in public, send sweet texts, and made me feel like I actually mattered.

But my past trauma still lingered.

One night, when he kissed me, I froze. Memories of that night with Kash flooded back, paralyzing me. He felt me tense up and pulled back instantly.

"You okay?" he whispered, concern etched on his face. I nodded too quickly.

"Yeah… yeah, I'm good."

But I wasn't.

He searched my face, then said gently, "I love you, Amber. Like, for real."

My throat tightened. I almost told him everythin' right then, almost broke down and let it spill.

But instead, I swallowed the words and whispered, "I love you, too... but I can't."

He didn't push. He just nodded, respectin' my boundaries.

That was why I loved him. He gave me space even when he didn't understand why I needed it.

The next afternoon, I decided to walk to the corner store to clear my head. My heart was still heavy from the night before, replayin' Rachelle's MySpace cut-off over and over.

As soon as I turned the corner, there she was—Rachelle—posted up with her brothers and a couple of their homeboys. They were laughin' loud, actin' bold like they owned the whole block. Our eyes locked. Rachelle smirked, and that was all it took for my chest to tighten.

She started talkin' loudly so everyone could hear.

"Look at her!" Thinkin' she all that now. Miss sympathy herself."

One of her little cheerleaders chimed in, "Girl, you ugly!" Then they all burst out laughin' like it was the funniest thing in the world.

My face stayed stone cold.

On the outside I looked unbothered, but inside? My heart was poundin' so loud it felt like it was in my throat.

I knew then that me and Rachelle were gonna fight.

Maybe not today, maybe not tomorrow, but eventually. Too much fake love had built up between us for it to go any other way.

I didn't give her the satisfaction of a response.

I just turned around, held my head high, and walked off.

I was boilin' inside.

While I was walkin' home, I thought about how tired I was of fake friends, tired of lies, tired of the constant battles.

Truth was, I never had a mother to run to. Michelle was never really a mama to me.

She treated me like I was just another girl off the street, not her own child.

My siblings? They were scattered, barely around.

And Daddy… even when he was free, he was cold. Angry. More of a drill sergeant than my father. Love from him felt like a test I was always failin.'

Granny was the only one who truly tried to hold me down, the closest thing I had to a best friend. But even she didn't always understand me.

Her love was real, but sometimes it came with rules and expectations I couldn't meet.

That was why losin' Rachelle hurt so much.

I didn't just see her as a friend; I saw her as family.

When I let someone get close, I gave them my whole heart. So, when they turned on me? It cut deeper than any fist fight ever could.

Most of the girls I tried to be cool with were fake, jealous, or just users.

They liked my shine, liked the way I carried myself, but they didn't really love me. Not for me.

It felt like everywhere I turned; somebody was tryna dim my light.

Standing outside that store, I realized Rachelle wasn't just a friend actin' funny; she was another person showin' me who they really were.

Later that night, the house phone rang. It was Granny; her voice was soft but tired.

"Baby," she said. "They keepin' me overnight. I'll be home tomorrow. You holdin' it down?"

"Yes, ma'am. I love you," I told her, my voice crackin.'

"I love you, too, baby," she whispered.

Hearin' her voice gave me a sense of calm like a warm blanket around my heart.

I started singin' on the phone until my granny fell asleep; she loved when I was soft and sweet.

Minutes later, the phone rang again. This time, it was Daddy.

"Amber." Just that one word, sharp and heavy. His voice was rough and low, filled with anger not at me exactly, but at the world. "You takin' care of the house? Don't let nobody in. You hear me? Nobody."

"Yes, sir," I answered.

"Call Raymond if you need groceries. And Amber... you gotta be strong. For Mama. For yourself."

Before I could say anythin' back, he hung up.

I sat there holdin' the phone, my hand still warm from the call, wishin' he could be the daddy I needed. But deep down, I knew he wasn't that man.

That night, I sat in my room starin' at the ceilin,' thinkin' about everythin': Granny in the hospital, Daddy locked up, Mama gone, Rachelle turnin' on me.

I felt like the whole world was against me.

But I also felt a spark deep inside, small but fierce.

I grabbed my journal and wrote:

"I'm done lettin' people play with me. Done lettin' life break me down. I'ma find my voice, my strength, my freedom. Even if I gotta do it alone."

As I closed the journal, I wiped my tears and whispered to myself, "I'm done playin' small."

And for the first time in my life, I believed it.

This was the beginnin' of me growing into myself.

Of seein' people for who they truly were, even when it hurt.

The fight with Rachelle was comin,' sure, but the real battle wasn't with her.

It was with the world. With the pain I carried.

With learnin' how to stand tall when everythin' around me was tryna pull me down.

CHAPTER FIVE

WHEN INNOCENCE WAS INTERRUPTED

The silence, the shame, and the secret I carried alone.

That summer was different. I was older now but still stuck in the middle of my childhood and a fast-track adulthood I didn't ask for. My daddy still locked up, my granny still dealin' with her health, and me? I was just tryna survive it all and still figure out who the hell I was.

It was hot as hell in Oakland; sun beamed down on the cracked sidewalks and loud kids runnin' wild in the street. I landed me a little job bussin' tables at this soul food spot downtown with low pay, but it gave me something to do. Somethin' to keep my mind off the past and everythin' I was carryin' that I didn't know how to let go of. I was still grievin,' still bruised from what Kash did to me.

In between shifts and fryin' chicken at home, I was tryna catch up on school. I had to go to summer school at Skyline High. I was behind in math and credits. I had to catch up if I was ever gonna step foot in the 8th grade and finally be high school bound.

But walkin' through them hallways wasn't easy. The same girl I fought before, the one I laid out like a welcome mat, was there with her little crew. Every time they saw me, they'd roll their eyes, whisper loud on purpose.

"There go that bald-headed ugly girl with the manly face."

"Girl look like she got more facial hair than my daddy."

I heard all of it. They made sure I did.

What made it worse was… some of it felt true.

See, Nikki, this woman my daddy used to mess with, took out my hair one day, claimin' she was gon' redo it. She damn near left me bald. Didn't even try to fix it up. I looked in the mirror and didn't recognize myself. I wasn't dusty, nah. My clothes was clean. I stayed fresh as I could, but I ain't have no Jordans or Apple Bottoms or none of that fly stuff all the other girls had. My granny wasn't hipped to none of that. She did what she could with what she had. Walmart, Mervyn's, sometimes Ross if we got lucky. But you know kids, if it ain't designer they thought it was trash.

Still, I kept my head up, even when it felt heavy.

I had this big-ass forehead I used to hate, facial hair that made me insecure, and a body that was developin' faster than I was mentally ready for. Puberty had me in a chokehold. I was confused and emotional all the time. I ain't know what was wrong with me. I'd lash out, cry for no reason, argue with my granny like she was my little sister. She didn't understand. She'd yell; I'd yell back. And then I'd slam the door and cry into my pillow like I didn't have no one in the world.

And sometimes… that was how it felt.

So, I pushed through. I tried to find moments of peace where I could. Some days, I'd just sit outside and let the sun hit my skin, headphones in, Fantasia or Keyshia Cole on repeat. Their songs knew what my soul felt before I could even say it out loud.

At school, I kept it cute and quiet. I wasn't tryna fight no more. I just wanted to pass, elevate, and stay out the way. But every once in a while, that old anger would bubble up when folks pushed me too far.

One day after class, I was walkin' through the quad and caught one of the girls from the crew starin' at me.

"What you lookin' at?" I said without even thinkin.'

She smirked. "Just tryna figure out if that's a mustache or a shadow."

My fists clenched. I had to take a deep breath and keep walkin.' I wasn't about to throw away my progress. I wasn't.

Later that day, I went home and stood in front of the bathroom mirror. I ran my fingers across my upper lip. Yeah, it was there. I got the tweezers and handled it best I could, but deep down, that little comment stuck with me.

I looked myself in the eyes. "You still beautiful," I whispered.

Even if nobody else said it, I had to.

In the 2000s, you could get a job young. I was barely thirteen and already hustlin' at this little soul food spot down on MacArthur. Mr. J ran it. He was a big, brown-skinned dude with silver caps on his back teeth, always smilin' and talkin' slick. He loved my granny, said she used to babysit him and his cousins back in the day, so he let me slide with the job. I wasn't officially old enough, but he was payin' me under the table $6.25 an hour, cash in hand, no questions asked.

The work was hard sometimes, but I felt grown. Cleanin' tables, runnin' orders, takin' phone calls, wrappin' to-go plates. It gave me somethin' to focus on instead of all the other shit I had been dealin' with. Every day I left that place smellin' like fried fish and collard greens, but I ain't care. I was gettin' money, and in my world that meant freedom.

When my birthday came, it felt like a tiny piece of joy in a life full of mess. Granny bought me a vanilla cake with whipped frosting and pink letters that said, "Happy Birthday, Amber." She gave me a card with a $20 bill folded inside and a lil roll of singles wrapped in a rubber band. Then she picked up a few of my girls: Creshae, Brielle, and this new girl named Tati to take us bowlin' and out to eat at Sizzler. Nothin' fancy, but we had fun.

That night, they all stayed over. We played cards, talked mess, ate on this big pot of Rotel dip my granny made with warm tortilla chips, and fruit salad on the side. She even made my favorite: that strong-ass blueberry lemonade Kool-Aid that had you puckerin' up after every sip. I remember just sittin' there, laughin,' watchin' *Set It Off* on VHS, feelin' like maybe, just maybe, life was about to get better.

But then reality always found its way back.

The rest of the summer came and went like a blur. I was still dealin' with my rape in silence. I didn't tell nobody, not even my closest girls. I ain't know how. I wanted to feel normal. So, I smiled when I needed to, laughed when I was supposed to, and kept it pushin.'

Then came 8th grade at Skyline. I ain't even want to go back. The whispers started first. Then the looks. Then the bold-ass comments. Everybody was sayin' I lost my virginity to Kash. That I was ugly. That I had a mustache and sideburns and a big-ass forehead. I'd walk through the hallway like I was invisible and loud at the same time. Kash had told everybody that he took one for the team. Said I was a manly bitch and that he should've passed. My stomach used to knot up every time I saw him.

One day, in science class, his alleged girlfriend at the time, Sanaa, turned around and asked me bold as hell, "So, you really fucked Kash?" My heart dropped. I could've lied. I could've stayed quiet. But instead, I looked her straight in her eyes.

"He raped me."

Her face changed instantly like her whole soul paused. She didn't say nothin' for a long moment. Then her eyes welled up with tears. "I didn't know..." she whispered.

She looked disgusted. Hurt. But even then, it didn't stop her from dealin' with him. She still walked the hallways holdin' his hand. Still sat next to him at lunch like I never said a word. And that crushed me in a way I didn't even know how to explain.

That year was hard. I was tryna keep my head on straight, make up my credits in summer school, and push through all the noise.

My hair was still a mess from that one time Nikki snatched my braids out and left me with bald spots. Daddy's side chick, one of them bitter-ass women he messed with, told her to do it. Said I had an attitude. All I had was trauma and nowhere to put it.

I was just tryna survive. *God, I need You*, I always thought.

I bowed down and reflected on the obstacles I'd overcame even with trials and tribulations; I kept the faith. All I could recite in my head was this scripture.

"When the righteous cry for help, the Lord hears and delivers them out of all their troubles,"

Psalm 34:17 (ESV)

God, where are You?

I sat in the dark corner of my room, huggin' my knees, cryin' so hard I couldn't breathe. My face was hot. My chest was tight. I wanted to scream so loud that the whole world would hear me. I wanted to disappear. I wanted to die.

It felt like no matter how hard I tried to keep my head above water, life kept pushin' me under. Everybody had somethin' to say about me. Everybody put a jacket on my back without ever askin' me what I'd been through or how I was really doing. Nobody knew my story. Nobody wanted to hear it. They just judged me. Laughed at me. Lied on me.

I was tired. So damn tired.

I was cryin' out to God in silence, but nothin' changed. I kept askin' Him, *why me? Why'd You pick me to carry all this pain? Why'd You give me parents who didn't know how to love me? Why didn't my family care? Was it because I wasn't light-skinned and pretty like the other girls? Was it because I came from nothin'? Was it because I didn't have the "perfect" family with Sunday dinners and bedtime stories?*

All I had was my granny. And as much as I knew she loved me, sometimes it just didn't feel like enough.

I cried and told her everythin' that was going on at school—the rumors, the teasin,' the name-callin.' I was tired of fightin' people every other week. I was tired of bein' the outcast. I was tired of bein' called ugly. I was tired of people talkin' about my facial hair, my forehead, the way I dressed.

She looked at me and said softly, "Amber, don't worry about what they say. You're not ugly. People talked about me in school, too."

But it wasn't the same.

I snapped. "It's not the same, Granny!" I shouted, tears streamin' down my face. "You don't understand! You don't get it! I'm tired of fightin.' I'm tired of bein' hated for no reason. Why did God give me these parents? Why don't I matter to anybody?"

My voice cracked. I was shakin.' "Why did God choose me to fight all these hard battles?! I didn't ask for this life! I didn't ask to be born into pain."

She stepped toward me and tried to wrap her arms around me, but I shoved her away with everythin' I had in me.

"I LOVE YOU, AMBER!" she screamed. Her voice cracked with frustration and pain.

And I screamed right back at her, "IT'S NOT ENOUGH!"

She stood there for a moment, her eyes full of sadness. She turned away, walked down the hallway, and slammed her bedroom door behind her.

I was left standin' there in the middle of the room, broken.

Just broken.

I dropped to my knees, cryin' out to God one more time. "Why did You make me like this? Why am I so hard to love?"

But even in the silence, I remembered that scripture my granny had underlined in her Bible.

"When the righteous cry for help, the Lord hears and delivers them out of all their troubles,"

Psalm 34:17

Maybe I didn't feel heard in that moment.

But maybe He heard me anyway.

The night air was thick in East Oakland. Muggy. It carried the sound of helicopters overhead, a few sirens in the distance, and the usual mix of neighbors talkin' loud and music playin' from somebody's Cutlass down the block. I stepped outside to get some air because I was trippin.' I knew I came at my granny foul, and deep down I knew she loved me, but this wasn't back in the day no more. Life was different. Harder. We needed real help, not just old-school wisdom and tough love.

It was like our family tree skipped a few branches when it came to supportin' us, especially me. My granny was everybody's favorite. Church folks loved her; the neighbors respected her. But me? I was just the daughter of the least favorite son, Thomas. And Michelle wasn't ever in the picture long enough to fight for me. It felt like I inherited both of their mess like bad karma ran through my veins. I was cursed from both sides.

For a while, I hated dudes. I thought they were disgustin.' I didn't trust them. Couldn't look at one without thinkin' about all the ways they'd hurt me physically, emotionally, and spiritually. Every time a dude looked at me, I saw danger. Disrespect. Control.

But at the *same time*, I needed them. That part was hard to admit, but it was real. I was still chasin' that love I never got from my daddy. That validation. That "you're beautiful," "you matter," "you're safe with me." I wanted to believe in it so bad.

I wanted to be like the girls in the movies—soft, held, kissed gently, loved loudly. I wanted that feelin.' That fantasy. But instead of love, I kept gettin' lessons. Painful ones. Ones that cracked me open.

I lost my daddy even if he was still breathin' behind them bars. Me and Granny was hangin' on by threads emotionally. Me and Rachelle? That fake friend stabbed me in my back so slick; I still felt it when I slept. My boyfriend? That clown played me for some light-skinned girl with a fat ass who ain't even pretend to be a virgin. School? They turned on me the minute my name was tied to Kash. The whole world was spinnin,' and I couldn't stop it. But I wasn't no punk. I'd always been a soldier. Another kid might've folded under this kind of pressure. But not me. I was off the porch. Now it was time to get it.

Another summer came and went. I made it through summer school barely. Still got them stares in the hallway at Skyline High—girls whisperin,' boys snickerin,' folks thinkin' they knew my story. That girl I fought? Her and her homegirls still called me ugly, talked about my face, my hairline, and my body. Like they was perfect. But I kept pushin.'

And then came the money issues. My daddy's house was about to be up for lien. Granny had been gamblin' heavy. She was chasin' dreams at the casino while bills sat on the counter unpaid. I started runnin' the streets more, not even out of rebellion, just survival. Sellin' weed. Flippin' pills. Workin' little under-the-table jobs at corner stores, hair shops, wherever they'd let me clock in and not ask questions. But it still wasn't enough. It never was.

And my daddy? Locked up and fightin' a damn murder charge for nearly beatin' a man to death. If that man died, they were trying for the death penalty. They broke both his ankles in prison just for not walkin' fast enough. Called him all types of racial slurs and when he fought back, they added more time—another two years on top of what he already had. His chick, Dejah, and some new girl, Lauriel, were sendin' him money and holdin' him down on his books and calls. Not me. Not his daughter. He barely mentioned me in the calls unless he was mad at me or tellin' me what to do.

I didn't tell nobody, but I was drownin.' Drownin' in heartbreak, in shame, in anger. I didn't wanna die… but I didn't know how to keep livin' like this. I was too damn young for this kind of weight.

But I held on even if it was just by a thread.

And in that darkness, I cracked open my Bible and my eyes landed on this verse.

"The Lord will fight for you; you need only to be still," Exodus 14:14.

I read that and cried like a baby because I was tired of fightin.' Tired of defendin' myself, tired of explainin' myself, tired of bein' the strong one when nobody gave me the space to fall apart.

That was when I realized, maybe I wasn't just survivin' for me… maybe I was survivin' for the girl I'd become. For the legacy I'd break. For the shift I was born to make.

But that was the thing about pain, it didn't always fade. Sometimes, it just made you sharper.

The summer heat in California was hittin' just right that day. Me and my girls—Brielle, Creshae, and Tati—decided to hit up this water park a couple cities over. I couldn't even lie, we was cute as hell in our little two-pieces, matchin' shades, and them $20 sandals from Below-The-Belt. That store stayed comin' through with the deals. You ain't gotta spend a lot to look good, and baby we knew how to make cheap look bomb.

I had my swoop ponytail laid, edges slicked with brown gel from a little toothbrush. My belly button was pierced, and I was feelin' grown and fine. My confidence that day? On a hundred. For once, I wasn't thinkin' about the drama, my pops locked up, or Rachelle's shady ass. I was just happy. Free. Laughin' with my girls and soakin' up the sun.

The slides were big and fast; me and Brielle screamed like we was on a rollercoaster. The lazy river was hittin,' too. We was posted up, floatin' in them inner tubes, legs hangin' off the side, water glistenin' on our skin like we was in a summer teen movie. Boys kept walkin' by in their Polo swim trunks, lookin' our way. Some of them were kinda fine too, tryna splash us and ask us our names. We giggled, flirted a little, then floated off like it was nothin.' Vibes all day.

My granny, bless her heart, was off to the side talkin' everybody to death like always. That woman could strike up a conversation with a tree. She always meant well though, and somehow, she managed to find her some card buddies and was sittin' at a table talkin' and laughing loud.

"Ay, Amber! Brielle! Creshae! Tati! Y'all come on, let's eat lunch!" Granny yelled, wavin' her hand like it was the last call at the lunch line.

We all hopped out the lazy river, slidin' our wet feet into our sandals, still drippin' wet. Our towels were barely dry, but we were hungry. We rushed to the shaded food court, plates loaded with pepperoni pizza, some bomb crispy crinkle-cut fries, and each of us had a large Sprite with crushed ice. That food hit like it was catered by God. We sat under one of those blue and yellow umbrellas and just vibed—talkin' about boys, what school was finna be like, who we had a crush on, and what we was wearin' for the first day.

Time flew. The sun started slidin' behind the clouds, and we knew it was time to pack up. We changed our wet clothes, grabbed our bags, and started headin' back to the parkin' lot.

And that was when I saw her.

Rachelle.

She was walkin' with some girls from her block, smirkin' when she spotted me. I locked eyes with her. All that fun I had just melted off me. The air felt heavy. Her little crew tried to play like they wasn't scared, but I saw the nervous look in her eye. Still, she played bold.

"What's up, Amber?" she said with that fake lil smirk like she ain't been the one throwin' dirt on my name.

"Nah, what's up with *you*? Heard you out here tellin' folks I lied about what happened to me," I said, steppin' closer.

"Girl, ain't nobody worried about you. I said what I said. You be lyin.' You just mad 'cause your man was choosin.'"

Before she could finish her sentence, I blacked out.

I charged at her. Hair flyin.' Arms swingin.' It wasn't no screamin,' no threats—just straight action. Years of pain, betrayal, humiliation, and heartbreak all poured out of me in that one fight. I snatched a whole chunk of her weave out, tracks in my hand like receipts. She scratched my face, but I caught her with a clean jab to her eye and blackened it. She came back and split my lip open. We was rollin' on that hot concrete, blood and tears everywhere, our homegirls screamin' tryna pull us apart. My granny ran over, her flip-flops smacking' loud, yellin' at the top of her lungs.

But I couldn't hear nothin.' My heart was beatin' loud in my ears. All I could see was her face and everythin' she took from me—my trust, my name, my peace. There wasn't no comin' back from that.

She had told people I was lyin' about being raped. Told folks I made it up for attention. She talked behind my back, flirted with my boyfriend, and smiled in my face like we were cool. But she was a snake. A coward. She was never my friend, and I should've seen it from the start.

That was the end of that.

Rachelle was officially dead to me. No more mercy. No more hope of fixin' anything. She showed her true colors, and I made sure she never forgot the day she tried the wrong one.

The summer ended with blood, sweat, and tears.

But trust me… that was just the beginnin.'

I wish I could go back to that little girl, the one sittin' there wonderin' why her mama never stayed and tell her it wasn't her fault. That love ain't supposed to leave bruises or disappear when the door closed.

I used to wonder if somethin' was wrong with me… like I was born too broken to be loved right. But now? I know I was just a child. A child born into a storm that wasn't mine to fix.

I grew up bein' hard on myself just as much as my father was hard on me. I thought if I was better, quieter, stronger, maybe then they'd love me the way I needed them to.

But I know now… I needed softness. I needed safety. I needed somebody to say, "you deserve joy, baby."

I laughed sometimes. I smiled sometimes. There were good moments tucked in between the pain. But even those moments had shadows.

If I could go back, I'd give that little girl an imaginary friend. Someone to walk her through tears. Someone to hold her hand through every disappointment.

Perhaps that's who I am now—the woman I once longed for.

CHAPTER SIX

SEEING IT FOR WHAT IT WAS

No More Sugarcoating. No More Pretending. This Was The Truth.

I was quiet because if I spoke the truth, it would hurt more than it would help. That was the sad part. My silence wasn't peace; it was survival. Every word I swallowed turned into weight on my chest. Sometimes, I felt like if I opened my mouth, everythin' would come pourin' out, and once it did, I wouldn't be able to stop.

But it wasn't all bad. I had real moments that gave me life, too. In my world history and math classes, I had a group of friends who cracked jokes all period long. They'd tell the funniest stories, some made no damn sense, but I laughed hard anyway. That laughter was a break from all the whispers and side-eyes. For fifty minutes at a time, I could forget the heaviness and just *be a kid*.

After school, we'd mob down that hill in a big ass pack, linkin' up with our other homegirls and homeboys from different hallways. We'd shoot the shit for a minute, act a fool, then go our separate ways. Some of us lived in the same neighborhood, so after we went home, chilled, and ate, we'd all come back outside and be out there for hours—talkin,' clownin,' vibin' about everythin' and nothin.'

We played freeze tag, slap boxin,' hide n'go get it—we had no business playin' that one. Sometimes we'd be out all night in front of somebody's house—dancin,' jokin,' catchin' a lil' vibe under the streetlights. I remember the kickbacks and house parties, too. Man, there was nothin' like them. Even if some of those folks ended up fake as hell later, those nights? I can't lie; I had hella fun. I needed that fun. I cherished those times even if they didn't last forever.

But the joy didn't erase the pain.

The next morning, I woke up feelin' like I got jumped by life itself. My lip looked like a busted-up sausage, all swollen and crusty. My arms were sore, my back ached, and my hands were stiff from how hard I had swung on Rachelle. It felt like I got hit by a truck in my sleep.

I took some Tylenol for the swellin' and tried to chill, but the mirror kept throwin' my reflection back at me. And it wasn't just bruises I saw, it was all the stuff I'd been holdin' in. Every fight left marks you couldn't see, too. Fear that people would always betray me. Shame that I couldn't stop the rumors. Anger that never seemed to leave my body. Nights I laid awake feelin' like I had to fight in my dreams, too.

My granny was quiet that morning. Hurt, disappointed, just pacin' and breathin' heavy like she was tryin' not to snap. She said she wanted to talk to Rachelle and her people. "Y'all was like sisters," she said, shakin' her head. "Lettin' a boy come between y'all like this?"

But it wasn't just about a boy. It was about betrayal. Loyalty. Principle. Rachelle was never really my friend, and that became really clear the moment she chose the streets over me. My name was in everybody's mouth. Lies on top of lies. Rumors that wouldn't stop. I was one of the most hated girls on the westside of Oakland and I hadn't even done half the things people said I did. They couldn't stand how I still held my head up, even when I felt like I was losin' every damn day.

Then came Johnthan, still lyin,' still playin' dumb like he ain't been talkin' to Rachelle. We got into it again, this time it was louder, messier. I told him I was done. He tried to flip it on me, like I was trippin' over nothin.' Boy, bye. I was tired of cryin' over someone who couldn't even keep it real. We broke up that night, and he still never owned up to what he did.

But what hit harder than all that was the fact that my "friends" started cliquin' up with my enemies. The same girls I used to share snacks with, walked home with, and cried to was now laughin' and smokin' with the same people who hated me. That crushed me. I'm big on loyalty. I don't play about that. If you're my friend, then my enemies are your enemies. Period. That's law.

Summers in Oakland got even hotter. Rumblings in the streets, Bloods and Crips beefin,' hood politics creepin' into teenage lives. Fights broke out at the corner stores, parks, and schoolyards. You had to stay ten toes down or get caught slippin.' It was rumble after rumble, and I was right in the middle of it.

But the truth? Half the time, I wasn't just fightin' them. I was fightin' myself. I'd go home after swingin' and felt hollow. Like I won the fight but lost a piece of me. Every rumor, every betrayal, every punch I threw chipped away at me inside. But I didn't know how to stop goin,' givin' up wasn't in me. I only knew survival. And survival looked like fists, hard faces, and silence when I was breakin.'

Granny couldn't take it no more. She sat me down one night, eyes watery but strong.

"You need a break," she said. "I'm goin' to New York to visit my sister, and you gon' stay with Auntie Nique for a while."

I ain't argue. I was tired. As much as I loved my granny, I couldn't move how I needed to around an old lady. I needed space. I needed to breathe.

So, I packed my bags and went to stay with Auntie Nique, my cousin Bri, and my boy cousin, Chase. It was different over there, a whole new energy. It was still in Cali, but far enough to feel like I was somewhere else. My auntie had more patience, Bri was like a sister, and Chase? That was my dog. We had each other's back through it all.

But the truth was I needed things—a cell phone, Sidekicks, name plates, Jordans, gold earrings, fresh clothes, new rings. I wanted to feel like somebody. And Granny's little SSI check wasn't stretchin' far enough to keep me laced. So, I did what I felt like I had to.

I started stealin.'

A little here, a little there. Lip gloss from Walgreens. Earrings from the beauty supply. Clothes out the mall with stolen tags. I was hustlin' on the side too, still sellin' a little weed and pills, doin' hair, and workin' under the table. I did anything I could to get my hands on the things I wanted. It wasn't glamorous, but it was survival.

Real talk, I thank God I never ended up in juvie or locked up, 'cause there were plenty times I should've been sat down.

It was survival of the fittest. But deep down, I hated that version of myself. Every time I slid somethin' in my bag, every time I lied about where money came from, I felt that little sting of guilt. I just shoved it down. I told myself I didn't have the luxury of guilt. I had to eat; I had to look like I belonged. Still, when I laid down at night, I'd wonder if I was disappearin' piece by piece, becomin' somebody I wouldn't even recognize.

Me and my cousin shared a room, and we had that sisterly vibe—laughin' until the late hours, whisperin' secrets, talkin' about boys, school, and everythin' in between. For a minute, it felt like a soft landin' like I could breathe again.

Meanwhile, Granny had made it safely to New York. First thing her and my aunt did was cook soul food and broke out the spades table. They had them oldies blastin'—The Temptations, Aretha, Patti LaBelle—and they were laughin' like teenagers again. When she called me, her voice was light, full of joy.

"Amber, baby, we just made smothered chicken and greens and started up a card game. I needed this."

I smiled through the phone. "I'm glad you're happy and at peace. I'm good, Granny. I promise I'm gonna go to school every day."

And I meant it. At least at the time.

Me and my cousins had hella fun together. We'd play video games all day, roast each other, and share childhood stories. For the first time in a long time, I felt like I was makin' good memories. I even met this boy named DJ. He was brown skinned, had deep waves, smelled like soap and cologne. He had this easy smile that made the weight on my chest feel lighter. We'd sneak off behind the pool house, kiss under the streetlights, or go swimmin' in the afternoons when nobody was watchin.'

But even in those sweet moments, reality never stayed away too long. My money was short, my granny was gone, my daddy was locked up, and my mama was still missin' in action. I was still just a kid carryin' grown people's weight on my shoulders.

One night, I stayed out way too late with DJ. We were laid up on this bench by the complex, talkin,' kissin,' laughin' like life wasn't heavy. Then I heard my auntie's voice rip through the night like thunder.

"Amber! Where the fuck you at?!"

She stormed the courtyard with a belt in one hand and a switch in the other. My cousins were beggin' her not to hit me. "Mama, please! She's not even that late!" But TT wasn't hearin' it. She was cussin,' pacin,' swingin' her fist into her palm like she was warmin' up to lay into me.

I ran around the back, tried to sneak through the alley, but she caught me. She raised her hand, and for a split second, I froze but then somethin' in me snapped.

"You not my mama! Don't be tryna put your hands on me like that!"

Her eyes went wide. The silence after that was louder than her screamin' had been. For weeks, she barely spoke to me. The house felt heavy with that quiet like walkin' through a fog.

But even with the tension, I kept my promise. I went to school every single day. I slowed down on the stealin' and hustlin not because I turned angel overnight, but because I knew if I pushed my TT one more inch, she'd put me out. She told me straight up, "I love you, Amber, but I got kids, too. If you can't get it together, you gotta go."

So, I got it together enough to stay.

Months passed before Granny came back. TT finally told her, "Look, I'm struggling. This girl needs you. She listens to you different." My TT moved in with me and my granny. Her and TT clashed over everythin' from bills to groceries—petty little things that stacked up. Our house became a war zone of whispers, slammed doors, and long sighs.

And on top of all that, I was broke but still hustlin.' It was a cycle I couldn't escape. I hated it, but survival didn't wait on morals.

The summer came so quickly with all the sudden changes in my life and growin' up so fast. By the time I looked up, I was in high school. I went to one of the worst schools in Oakland.

High school was its own battlefield. I got teased hella bad for being hairy. "She got a mustache," "That's a boy." The worst part? The girls joined in with the boys, laughin' like it was entertainment. Every word was a punch to my confidence.

But I wasn't weak. I fought back the only way I knew how—with my mouth. I became the baggin' queen, roastin' people so bad they'd leave in tears. Folks learned quick not to play with me. I wasn't lookin' for fights, but I finished them.

Still, behind all that loudness, I was bleedin' inside. Every joke, every fight, every rumor had stacked on me. Some nights, I'd stare at the ceilin' and wondered if people could tell how tired I really was. How much I wanted just one safe place.

At home, Granny was strugglin,' too. I remember one day walkin' in on her crying after a call with my daddy. They were goin' back and forth about me, about money, about everythin.' She was breakin,' and my daddy was blamin' me for how my granny was feelin.'

He told her I needed the military, that she was spoilin' me and settin' me up to fail. That day, he basically disowned me. The calls stopped after that. Granny was heartbroken, but she never told me to stop bein' me. Even in disappointment, she stood by me.

I kept movin.' Fake friendships came and went. I still got caught up in drama behind dudes, girls hatin,' boys playin' both sides. It was messy. But then somehow, me and Rachelle started talkin' again. Not all at once just a slow, cautious rebuild.

Her family was dysfunctional as hell. Everybody knew everybody's business, but nobody said a word. Her mama worked at a hotel but also turned tricks on the side of town in Oakland where the prostitutes be, but it stayed unspoken. I had a few homegirls that I hung with outside of prostitution who got down; I was no blonde to the game, I just wasn't a player. But let me be real… I wasn't blind to the game. I had friends who went that route. Girls I really loved who let older niggas lace them with shoes, phones, hair money, even rent. They weren't weak. They were just tired of bein' broke. Tired of beggin.' Tired of waitin' on miracles. So, when them shiny cars pulled up slow, windows cracked, "Come here, lil mama…" They listened.

I listened, too. Just not the same way.

These men would pull up on me the same way—suits, gold chains, cigarettes hangin' off they lip like they owned the pavement. They'd lean on the hood like they interviewin' me for a job I never applied for. "I can put you on, baby. You too pretty to be strugglin.' You sittin' on gold and don't even know it."

I just looked at them. Blank face. No smile.

They thought I was shy, but I was calculatin.'

I knew what they really meant. It wasn't hustle. It was ownership.

They didn't want to help me. They wanted to brand me.

And that was when I shut it down real quick. "I just wasn't that girl. I rather sell dope before I gave up my pussy," I would tell them.

They never expected me to say it out loud. Some walked off mad. Some laughed like I was stupid for choosin' struggle over "security."

But fuck it. I wasn't sellin' my body for anybody's dream but mine.

Truth be told though... I ain't gonna sit here and act holy. I used to joke with my homegirls like,

"But if a Charlie Wilson ever came my way and funded my life, I just might..."

And we'd crack up, 'cause we knew the difference.

A *pimp* wanna own you.

A *sponsor* wanna see you win.

And until God sent me that sponsor, I'd keep hustlin' on my own terms even if it meant late nights, empty pockets, and pride as my only paycheck.

Back to Rachelle. Her brothers were a mix. Antwan tried to act like her daddy, loud and controllin'; Tay Bird, quiet but didn't play; the youngest, square but with real hands.

It wasn't perfect, but me and Rachelle got cool again. We went to parties, mall runs, and movie nights. Her family slowly warmed back up to me. I kept my guard up, though. Once you crossed me deep, I never forget.

Meanwhile, Granny's health was declinin.' She was coughin' heavy at night, wheezin' like every breath cost her. I'd knock on her door and ask, "You good, Granny?"

"Yes, baby, I'm fine."

"You need anything?"

"No, baby, I got it, Pooh."

She always tried to play strong, but I could see right through it.

Through all of this, I was still tryna find myself. I kept my hair fresh in individuals twists by my own hands, neat and tight. I even got braces, tryna glow up. Boys came and went, but nothin' ever stuck. I wanted love, but I didn't know what real love even looked like.

Then came prom. Granny made sure I had the best night possible. She paid for everythin,' no hesitation. I went with my boy, Lavelle, my real friend. He pulled up in a crisp tux with a fresh lineup. I wore a fitted white pearl dress, bone-straight weave flowed down my back, silver heels, and my braces shined when I smiled. We looked like we stepped out of a music video.

That night, we danced, laughed, and ate good. Our double-date couple was a mess. The girl passed out drunk while her date kept eatin' like nothin' happened. Me and Lavelle couldn't stop laughin.'

By the time he dropped me off, I was dead tired. I peeled out of my dress, showered, then collapsed in bed. For one night, I felt like a regular teenage girl.

But life didn't let me have joy too long. Finals came, and I passed everythin' but math. I failed that exam twice. Still, I showed up every single day. Hoodie on, headphones in, journal open. Teachers said I was smart but disconnected. They didn't know I was survivin,' not learnin.'

Graduation came. I wasn't walkin' with a diploma yet, just completion of attendance but that stage meant everythin.' It meant I survived. Granny cried seein' me in cap and gown. My family packed the crowd deep.

And then him.

My daddy.

Standin' by the fence—fresh white tee, arms folded—eyes scannin' until he locked on me. My stomach dropped. I hadn't seen him since I was twelve. Six years gone, missed everythin.' Now, here he was paroled—free.

I didn't know how to feel. Mad? Happy? Numb? All of it at once?

And then his girl, Barbra, built like she benched buses, face screwed up like sour lemons looked me up and down like competition. This wasn't about her.

He walked up slow. "Amber..."

My mouth was dry, my chest heavy.

"Hey," I said. No hug. Just space and silence. Granny pulled me close. "She did it. Our baby did it."

Barbra tried to chime in, "Congratulations, sweetie." I cut her with a look.

After the ceremony, we took pictures, I laughed with Lavelle, classmates hugged me, but I still couldn't shake it. My daddy was back. No letters, no calls; he just showed up.

Later that night, Granny sat with me in the kitchen over leftover caramel cake.

"What's next, baby?" she asked.

"I'm going to adult ed. Finish that last math class. Pass that proficiency. Get my diploma."

I wasn't lettin' anything stop me. Not after everythin' I'd been through.

Daddy said he wanted to take me to dinner, just us. I didn't answer. Too much unfinished business. But deep down, I wanted to hear him out. Maybe for closure. Maybe for peace. Maybe for me.

One thing was certain, though; I wasn't the same girl he left behind. I was stronger, sharper, harder. I earned my place on that stage.

And I wasn't done yet.

CHAPTER SEVEN

WHEN IT ALL FELL APART

*Hitting bottom with no safety
net but still breathing*

Dinner at the five-star spot in Oakland felt like a movie. My curls were laid, my fit was fire, and my energy was finally light for once.

I walked in with my head high, feelin' grown, dressed in white like I had just baptized my damn past. Granny was glowin,' proud as hell, and my daddy… man, I hadn't seen him in six years, but there he was sittin' across from me like time ain't rob us blind.

I graduated high school and Thomas had missed some significant milestones in my life. I'd changed and so had my feelings toward him. Between me and you, I felt good he showed up for me in this moment… Granny had been a real one; she was more excited for me than I was for myself.

He had on a clean polo shirt, extra ironed jeans, and some beat-up sneakers that told me he was still tryna get back on his feet. That buff broad sittin' next to him, Barbara, yeah, she was thick and heavy in the face, loud laugh, cheap lip gloss, definitely not what I imagined he'd bring around. But whatever. I peeped game and kept it cute.

My aunties, cousins, even some folks I ain't seen since middle school pulled up to the restaurant. We talked about my next moves—college, life, and my dreams. I told 'em about University of Austin Texas. They gasped like I said Harvard or somethin.' But they were proud. Even though I walked across that stage with completion of attendance instead of a full diploma, I knew I earned every bit of that applause.

After dinner, I kissed my granny on her cheek and dipped out the back with a couple homegirls to meet up with the crew at the bowling alley by the movies. The parkin' lot was packed. There was laughter, music from car speakers, somebody smokin' loud—it smelled like teenage rebellion and cheap cologne. That was when I saw him. Jabari.

He was posted with a few of the homies near the side gate, leanin' on the meter box like he owned the block. He wore a black tee, Levi jeans, and a fresh taper. He wasn't no showstopper in the looks department, but his confidence always made him stand out. He was the type to hold the door for you, tell you you're beautiful without tryna holla, and that night it hit different. His smile pulled at me.

"Ayo, Amber," he said, walkin' over with that familiar swagga. "You lookin' like you runnin' this whole city tonight."

I chuckled, twirled my wrist, and shot him a grin. "I always been that girl. You just now noticin?'"

We both laughed. I leaned up on the pole, arms crossed, tryna keep it cool, but the way he looked at me made me feel seen, like really seen. Not for my body, not for the rumors or the street talk, just for me.

He said, "You still on the west with your granny?"

"Yeah, she knocked out in my daddy room. Pops already flew back to Arizona." I said it nonchalant, but there was weight behind those words. My father was barely out and already dipped again. Typical.

"You tryna chill for a lil bit?" I asked, bitin' my lip just a little. I wasn't tryin' to play games.

He paused. "You sure?"

I nodded and led him down the block. We slid into the house—quiet, lights low, the hum of a fan spinnin' in the hallway. Granny's door was shut. I peeked inside. She was out cold, snorin' softly, curled on the edge of my dad's old bed, TV flashin' on low. I closed the door gently and led Jabari to my room.

It wasn't much—just a mattress, my mirror lit up with dollar-store lights, and posters of Aaliyah and Monica on the wall. I lit my incense, sprayed my little room mist, and turned on some slow jams in the background. I told him sit down and make himself at home.

He kicked off his shoes and sat on the edge of my bed, lookin' nervous but tryna hide it.

"So, what's next for you, Miss Graduate?" he asked, lockin' eyes with me.

I shrugged and climbed onto the bed next to him, legs tucked under me.

"Tryna get this damn diploma. Then maybe Texas. I'm done lettin' people think I ain't shit. I know what I'm worth now."

He nodded slow, like he was really listenin.' "I always knew you was different. I just ain't know if I was your type."

I smirked, leaned in close. "What's my type, Jabari?"

He bit his bottom lip, voice droppin' low. "Somebody real. Somebody who ain't gon' fold."

We sat there in that moment so quiet, so heavy with everythin' unspoken. Then I leaned in, and we kissed. Slow. It wasn't just about lust. It was about bein' seen, touched gently after so much pain. I ain't let it go far. I wasn't ready for all that, but that kiss. It was grown. It was a new chapter.

My phone buzzed with texts from the crew outside askin' where I went, but I ain't care. That moment was mine.

For the first time in a long time, I wasn't rushin' to escape my life; I was finally startin' to live in it.

October rolled around, and the air started changin.' The Bay always got that crisp cool breeze that let you know fall was creepin' in. I had just turned eighteen. No big party, no cake with candles, none of that extra— just me, in my room, sittin' on the edge of my bed thinkin' 'bout everythin' I'd done seen and survived to make it here.

That night felt slow. Quiet. The kind of quiet where your thoughts started echoin.' I wasn't expectin' nothin' major, but then I heard that tap on my window, the soft double knock I knew was Jabari.

I cracked it open, and he was standin' outside, hoodie on, leanin' against the fence like he didn't wanna wake up the world. "You up?" he whispered.

I nodded and went to open the door for him. My granny was still out cold, knocked out in my daddy's room like always. I made sure the coast was clear, locked the front door, and led him back to my room.

He looked at me different that night. Not like the goofy, sweet Jabari from the bowling alley but more serious, focused. We sat close on my bed, knee to knee. I had on a big T-shirt and some shorts, my hair up in a messy bun, no makeup, no filter, just me.

"You ever think about… us?" he asked. I looked at him and blinked slow.

"Us how?"

He leaned in, brushed a strand of hair behind my ear, and said, "Like… bein' more than just cool."

I ain't say nothin.' I just stared at his soft lips. Familiar. Safe. I leaned in first. That kiss started out slow with soft pecks that turned into heavy breathin.' His hands started to explore, tracin' my thighs, then slidin' under my shirt. My chest rose up with nerves, but I ain't stop him.

His lips moved to my neck, then my collarbone. I tilted my head back, eyes flutterin,' but deep down, my heart was poundin' like a bass drum. This was new. My skin was tinglin' with anticipation and confusion at the same time. I wanted him, but I didn't know what was next.

He pulled his hoodie off, then his shirt. I laid back slowly as he climbed over me, eyes locked. I didn't ask him to stop. I didn't ask him to wait. He was the first boy to make me feel like I wasn't just some hard girl from the block. He made me feel wanted.

He reached for my shorts and slid 'em down. My legs shook a little. He kissed the inside of my thighs—slow, deliberate. I gasped. My hands gripped the blanket, and my eyes darted around the room like I was tryna find my senses.

Then I felt him press himself between my legs, the warmth of his skin against mine.

He didn't pull out a condom. I didn't ask. It happened so fast, but it also felt like time was movin' slow.

"You sure?" he whispered against my ear.

I nodded, even though my chest was screamin,' *I'm not ready*. But my lips didn't move. My body tensed as he guided himself in. The pressure was real. Painful. It felt like my whole body was bein' cracked open from the inside. He was rough, too rough, for it to be my first time. My eyes watered. I gritted my teeth.

"Damn… you tight," he whispered.

I hissed through my teeth. "Shh…"

I wanted it to feel beautiful like the way the movies made it look. But it wasn't. It was hot, uncomfortable, thick air filled the room, sweat mixed with nerves and confusion. He kept goin,' pushin' deeper, not really readin' my body. I think he thought I was lyin' about bein' a virgin… until the blood started to drip down my thighs.

He paused for a second. Looked down.

"Yo… forreal?"

I turned my head and stared at the wall. My chest felt heavy. I nodded.

He didn't say nothin,' just kept goin.' He was quick. Fast strokes like he was chasin' a nut, not makin' love. I laid there still, achin,' quiet.

In the middle of it all, he leaned in close and said, "You ever think about havin' my baby?"

I blinked. Did I just hear that?

I didn't answer. He came shortly after, breathin' heavy, body drippin,' then rolled off me. I laid there for a second, legs still open, blood and heat mixin' between my thighs.

He sat up, got dressed quietly, and then leaned down and kissed my forehead.

"Rest in peace to that lil' virginity," he whispered, half-laughin' like it was a joke.

I cracked a forced smile, then pulled my blanket over me. My throat burned. I felt like somethin' sacred had been taken not violently, but carelessly.

We tiptoed to the front door, his hand brushin' mine. Before he left, he turned and looked at me like he was tryna read my mind. I nodded and closed the door behind him.

Once he was gone, I walked slowly back to my room, wincin' with every step. I sat on the toilet and saw the streaks of blood. I cleaned myself up in silence.

That night, I didn't cry.

I just laid in my bed, starin' at the ceilin' fan, legs curled up, realizin' I wasn't the same no more.

Not a girl, not yet a woman. Just caught somewhere in between.

My granny ain't notice nothin.' She got up in the middle of the night to get some water like she always did, peeked her head in my room to check on me, then went right back to bed. She ain't think twice. I had the covers pulled up; pillow tucked just right like I was out cold. But inside I was wide awake, brain doin' laps, heart still racin' from everythin' me and Jabari had done. I laid there wonderin' what it all meant, if it even meant anything at all to him.

Days went by and he ain't call, not even a damn text. My nerves started eatin' at me, so I picked up the phone and called him. He answered after two rings like he wasn't even expectin' me.

"Hello," he said all nonchalant like I was just some random number poppin' up.

"Ugh... hey, Jabari."

"Wassup?"

"What you doing?" I asked, tryna sound chill but my voice was shaky.

He replied, "Why you ain't call me?"

"I was waitin' on you," I said softly. "I mean... you just took my virginity, and I been thinkin' about you."

He let out a half-laugh. "Is that right?"

"Yeah. You ain't thought about me?"

"Uhm... a little," he said like he was too busy eatin' or distracted.

I could hear him smackin' on food and guzzlin' water like I was interruptin' his damn dinner.

"Aye, let me call you back," he said quickly.

I paused, chest tightenin.' "Ok..." I said before hangin' up. I stared at my phone, screen dark, heart poundin' with disappointment.

This heavy ass feelin' settled in my gut like a warnin.' I tried to brush it off, but somethin' felt off. Like my spirit was vibratin' wrong.

I got up to go use the bathroom and the second I sat down on the toilet; I damn near jumped up screamin.' It burned bad like fire had lit my insides. I panicked and pulled my pants off fully, scratchin' like I had ants in my drawers. The itchin' was worse than anything I ever felt before. I snatched the shower curtain back, jumped in the water, as if that was gonna wash the confusion and fire away.

Under that hot stream, I scrubbed and scrubbed, washin' down there over and over, tryna make sense of what was happenin' to me. I didn't know if I was pregnant or if this was somethin' worse. I was a virgin before him; I didn't know how fast you could get pregnant or if this feelin' was normal. Was this what sex felt like after? Was this pain a part of it?

A small part of me, as scared as I was, started fantasizin' about being pregnant. I thought, maybe if I was... it'd be different. I'd be somethin' real. My friends already had babies, Rachelle had one, even though we wasn't talkin.' Two of my other homegirls had kids with their high school dudes. They always seemed so full of love, and I craved that. Even if it came from a place of brokenness, it was *theirs*. I wanted to feel needed, too.

But the thing was, I still felt like a virgin before Jabari. I ain't let Kash go all the way in. My legs were clamped so tight, he couldn't slide in. I remember the friction, the pain, his weight pressin' down on me while I screamed with my body and not my mouth. He didn't believe me when I said no, but I made sure he didn't penetrate me. It still counted as trauma, though, still counted as violation. Even if he didn't fully take me, he tried. That stayed in my body for years.

That was what made losin' my virginity to Jabari so heavy. It wasn't just sex; it was a piece of me I had never given up. And now he was actin' like I was just another name in his phone. My heart couldn't process it.

And my body? My body was screamin' at me louder than anything—itchin,' burnin,' achin' in places that had never ached before. I ain't know who to talk to. I didn't wanna tell my granny; she'd lose it. I damn sure couldn't tell no friends. They'd either laugh or judge.

I dried off in silence, wrapped in a towel and shame. My mind kept rewindin' to that night how I let him inside me without even askin' about protection. How he kissed me slowly, then turned savage and rough like he was tryna prove a point.

He ain't stop.

He ain't even ask if I was okay.

He just kept goin' till he nutted—quick—like I was a box to check off. And I took it.

I let it happen even though my heart wasn't all the way in it. I wanted him to love me. I wanted to feel chosen. And now I was left wonderin' if all I did was give him a story to laugh about with his boys.

I laid back in bed, legs pulled to my chest, starin' at the ceilin' like it had answers. The house was quiet, too damn quiet. My granny was in the next room, probably dreamin' about better days. And here I was... a grown ass girl who felt invisible.

The real pain? It wasn't even physical. It was in my soul.

Over the next few days, the pain became worse and so did the itchin.' I could barely sit down without feelin' like I was sittin' on a bed of fire ants. My underwear felt like sandpaper, and I was itchin' so bad; I wanted to scream. I tried takin' a bath, usin' soap, even baby wipes but nothin' helped. It was clear somethin' was off, and it wasn't goin' away on its own. I grabbed my little crossbody, put on some sweats, and made my way to the hospital. I was nervous as hell but too uncomfortable to care.

When I walked in, the nurse behind the counter barely looked up as she handed me the clipboard.

"Fill this out, sweetie," she said like she said that same line a hundred times a day.

I filled out the paperwork with a shaky hand. My name, date of birth, symptoms. I hesitated when it came to explainin.' My heart thudded as I scribbled down my symptoms. I turned it in and sat down, tryna keep myself from cryin' in public.

About fifteen minutes later, a triage nurse called my name. "Amber?"

I got up slowly, every step remindin' me that somethin' was wrong down there. I followed her to a little room where she took my vitals, checked my heart rate, and asked me some questions. I couldn't even focus. My mind was spinnin.'

She finished and gave me a tired smile. "Alright, the doctor will see you shortly, hun. Sit tight."

I waited about another thirty minutes before they called me back. I got put in a cold room with loud ass paper on the exam table that crinkled every time I moved. The door opened, and in came a doctor with kind eyes and gloves already on.

"So, Amber," she said, glancin' over my chart. "Tell me what's goin' on today."

I tried not to sound too embarrassed. "It burns when I pee. I'm itchy... real itchy. It hurts down there. And I think I might be pregnant."

She nodded slowly. "Okay. We're gonna take good care of you. I'm gonna give you some pills for the pain today. We'll run some blood work, a pregnancy test, and we're gonna do a vaginal swab to check for any infections or STDs. It might be a little uncomfortable."

A little uncomfortable was an understatement. When they did that culture test, I clenched the table so hard; my knuckles turned white. It felt like they was takin' pieces of me with that damn Q-tip.

Afterward, they had me pee in a cup and drew blood from my arm. I sat there waitin,' tryna tell myself this was all a part of the process. I wasn't sick. I was pregnant. Me and Jabari were gonna have a baby. A miracle baby. He asked me durin' sex if I wanted to have his kid. That had to mean somethin.' We was gonna build from this.

A nurse came back into the room, slidin' behind her little computer. "Okay, so... your pregnancy test came back negative."

My heart dropped.

Before I could even process that, she kept goin.' "And your vaginal culture tested positive for trichomoniasis."

Tricho-what?

She kept talkin,' but I couldn't hear her. The room started spinnin,' and it felt like the walls were closin' in. All I could think was, *How? What? Jabari?*

I left that hospital with a brown paper bag full of antibiotics, discharge papers, and a heart so cracked up, I didn't even feel like myself.

The minute I got home, I blew up his phone with calls and texts, back-to-back. No answer. For days. Weeks.

I had a bright idea. I blocked my number and called.

He answered.

"Hello?"

I tried to keep it together. "Ugh... hey, Jabari."

"Wassup?"

"What you doin'? Why you been ignorin' me?"

He paused like he ain't expect me to check him. "Why you ain't call me?"

"I did! I mean, you just took my virginity and I been thinkin' about you."

"Is that right?" He chuckled, smacking on food in the background like I wasn't sayin' nothin.'

"Yes. You ain't thought about me?"

He went quiet, then said, "Uhmm... a little."

That was when I heard a loud *gulp* like he was chuggin' down somethin.'

"Aye, let me call you back," he said all dry.

My heart dropped straight to my stomach. I wanted to go off, cuss his ass out, but I ain't wanna ruin nothin'... not yet.

"Okay," I whispered, and hung up.

I sat there itchin' and hurtin' feelin' dumb as hell. Finally, I couldn't take it no more. I called again. Blocked. He answered.

"What?" he said, all annoyed. I snapped.

"Why the fuck you ignorin' me? What did I do to you? You took my virginity."

"I don't know that."

I couldn't believe it. "Nigga, I was bleedin' and tight as hell."

"My dick big. That don't mean nothin.' Maybe I ain't pop your cherry."

I lost it.

"I just came from the fuckin' hospital. I'm pregnant."

He laughed.

I was stunned. "What's funny?"

"You," he said, still chucklin.' "I ain't even nut in you."

I felt the rage boil up in my chest. "You a bitch-ass nigga."

I hung up before I said somethin' worse. I slipped my shoes on so quick, they damn near flew across the room. I stormed out the front door, fists balled, heart shattered, eyes wet. I was headed straight to his house.

I didn't even stop to think; I just marched. Every step I took toward his house felt heavier than the last, but the fire in my chest pushed me forward. When I got to his block, I saw him outside, leanin' against the fence with a couple of his lil homies—laughin,' jokin' like life was sweet.

My heart damn near fell out my chest. I ain't even pause.

"Jabari!" I yelled, voice crackin' from the mix of pain and rage. He turned his head, saw me stormin' up, and that whole goofy-ass grin faded from his face like he already knew what was comin.'

— 79 —

He sucked his teeth, stood up straight, but didn't say a word.

"You really got me fucked up!" I snapped. "I let you in my body! My fuckin' soul! You took my virginity, and now you out here actin' like I don't even exist?!"

He squinted like my words was too loud for his ears. "Man, what is you even talkin' about?"

"You know exactly what I'm talkin' about! You ghosted me, made me feel like I meant somethin,' like we had somethin'... and then you gone act brand new?"

He shook his head, exhaled hard. "Amber... we not together. You actin' like we was in love or somethin.' I fuck with somebody else now."

And just like that, my stomach turned. It was like every part of me that still had hope dropped dead on the spot. My eyes burned, but I wouldn't cry not in front of him. Not after everythin' we've been through, not after everythin' he put me through.

"You fuck with somebody else?" I repeated slowly like I had to taste the poison before I swallowed it. "You couldn't even tell me that? But you was tryna make a baby with me, remember that?!"

He rolled his eyes then outta nowhere, he gripped his phone and *threw it*. That shit flew through the air, slammed on the concrete, and shattered like my fuckin' trust. The homies around him looked stunned, stepped back, not wantin' no parts of the drama.

"Nah, fuck all this!" he barked like *I* was the problem. "You trippin.' You blowin' this way outta proportion."

Way outta proportion?

I stood there, my jaw locked, chest heavin.' That was the moment. The *exact* moment the switch flipped in me. I felt myself go cold. Somethin' in me died that night, and it wasn't just the lil fantasy I had about love or first times or some happily ever after.

It was *me*—the soft, naïve version. She didn't make it past his sidewalk.

"Aight," I said quietly, steady. "I see you."

And I did.

From that night on, I moved different. The light in me dimmed, and the way I used to dream about bein' loved. That shit faded away. I grew numb. I stopped expectin' apologies, explanations, or closure. I realized Jabari ain't want me; he just wanted to be the first. He couldn't wait to hit so he could tell everybody. That was all I ever was to him.

Another story to brag about.

But me? I wasn't gonna let that be the end of my story.

I walked off that block heartbroken, but head held high. Because even if I was shattered, I'd rather piece myself back together alone than let somebody else break me twice. I got back home that night feelin' all types of ways—ashamed, angry, confused, and hurt. My chest was heavy, like somebody was sittin' on it. I went straight to my room, slammed the door shut, and pulled out my diary from under my pillow. That journal was the only place I could tell the raw truth without nobody side-eyin' me or twistin' my words. My pen hit that paper like a blade, slicin' through every emotion I had been tryna suppress.

"I gave myself to a nigga who ain't even care. I let my guard down, and now I feel violated all over again. Like I ain't learn nothin' from what Kash did. But this time I said yes, so now who do I blame? Me?"

I was writin' deep. Tears slid down my cheeks without warnin.' I wiped 'em away and looked up at my digital clock on the dresser. I blinked; it was 2:22 AM.

Something about that number hit different. I sat still, just starin' at it like it was talkin' to me. I grabbed my phone, wiped the screen, and looked up angel number 222. It said somethin' about balance, harmony, trustin' the process. That I needed to stop doubtin' myself and start trustin' the divine. That everythin' that was happenin' right now was a part of a bigger picture that I couldn't fully see yet. And I swear, it felt like God was speakin' directly to me.

I remembered the scripture I heard at church once, *"Trust in the Lord with all your heart and lean not on your own understanding. In all your ways acknowledge Him, and He shall direct your path,"* (Proverbs 3:5-6). That verse hit me deep in the soul. I'd been doin' things my way, leanin' on what I thought I knew, and look where that got me. Heartbroken, itchin,' and tryna piece myself back together.

I wrote that scripture at the top of the next page in bold letters. Then I wrote, *"God, I don't know what You got planned for me, but I'm tired of tryin' to force things that ain't for me. Please help me trust You."*

I closed my diary and leaned back against the wall. My stomach was still sore, and I had to keep takin' them damn antibiotics for the next seven days until this infection cleared up. Every time I took one, I felt like I was swallowin' disappointment. I wanted so bad to get Jabari outta my head, but it was like his name was stuck between my ribs.

So, I picked up my phone, hesitated for a second, then called one of my homegirls, Brielle. We hadn't been tight lately, but I needed to talk to somebody—anybody. My circle had been on some shady shit, hangin' with folks I didn't rock with, doin' grimy stuff behind my back. But I couldn't carry this weight alone.

When she answered, I took a deep breath and said, "I lost my virginity."

There was a pause on the line. Then she said, "Damn, girl… forreal?"

"Yeah… I thought he was different," I said, I was barely holdin' it together. Then I told her everythin' about the hospital, the STD, how Jabari ghosted me like I never mattered, and how I had tried to act strong, but I was breakin' down inside. She got quiet again, then she sighed really low.

"I'm sorry, Amber. For real. For not bein' there and for bein' fake with you before. I be goin' through my own shit too, but that's no excuse. I just be livin,' tryna have fun, not gettin' caught up in everybody else's drama… but I miss you. You forgive me?" Her voice cracked a lil.' That was when I knew she was serious.

"I miss you, too," I said. And I meant it.

Even though we hadn't been close lately, she listened. That was all I needed in that moment, somebody to hear me. Somebody to say I wasn't crazy for feelin' the way I did. I ain't have no siblings around to call. No mama to cry to. My dad? Back in Arizona on parole, ghostin' again. My granny? She cared, but she was the type to blow up before understandin' what was really goin' on. She'd make it about her, or worse, judge me and say I was fast or disrespectful. That was why I kept my shit private. My pain was mine, and mine alone.

But now… I was different. I felt my heart hardenin.' I wasn't the same soft girl I was a few weeks ago. That sweetness? Gone. I started movin' different. Talked less. Watched more. Every fake smile from a dude looked like a setup. Every girl who used to side-eye me, I was ready for 'em. Life had changed me.

But I knew one thing for sure, I wasn't gon' let this moment define me. Naw. I was gettin' back up. I was gonna heal. I was gonna go to school, chase somethin' real. I started lookin' into college again, thought about maybe even applyin' to that school in Texas I talked about. It wasn't over for me. I still had dreams. Still had goals. And God? He was still speakin.' I just had to keep listenin.'

After that fight with Jabari, I turned around and walked off, but inside I was boilin.'

I took the long way home, just me and the cement. Every step felt like another lie I had to carry. I was tired of bein' solid for people who folded on me.

I stopped at the corner store, got a Sprite, and some Hot Cheetos like that was gon' fix what I felt inside. It didn't.

When I got home, I sat in the dark for a minute, thinkin' about all the shit I been through. All the shit I survived. My chest started burnin,' and before I could stop it, I was cryin.' Not soft tears. That ugly, loud, whole-body cry.

I wasn't weak. But I was tired.

That night, I wrote on my wall with a black sharpie.

"You ain't gonna play me twice."

It was for everybody who thought I'd stay quiet. For Rachelle. For my daddy. For Kash. For all the fake friends and family who only loved me when it was convenient.

I wasn't playin' small no more. Not even a lil bit.

CHAPTER EIGHT

LIFE BE LIFE'N

The season where everything was just... heavy

...**B**ut that night, I sat in my room and wrote it all down. Every detail. Every feelin.' My diary was the only place I could bleed without *bleedin.'* I didn't think anybody would ever read it. It was mine. My truth. Until one day... it wasn't.

I found out Granny had read my diary. Not just read it, but shared some of my thoughts with the family and it got back to my daddy behind bars. My pain. My secrets. My voice laid out bare like I was some case study. That betrayal hit me harder than any ass whoopin.' I felt exposed. Violated. Like even the one person I trusted most had crossed a line that couldn't be uncrossed.

How could I ever write again after that?

How could I speak my truth if it was just gonna be passed around like gossip?

That was when I stopped writin' for a long time and stopped trustin' the people I loved the most.

I ain't gon' lie, after I got off that phone with Jabari, I ain't feel right.

Like somethin' inside of me cracked and leaked out. That boy took a piece of me and tossed it like trash. I sat on my bed in the dark, the only light was comin' from the cracked bathroom door. I had my diary in my lap, pen in hand, tryna write it all out but my fingers froze.

I looked up at the clock: 4:44 AM.

I blinked twice... then three times.

444.

Angel numbers. That was protection. That was my ancestors, my angels, the Most High watchin' over me sayin,' *'You're surrounded by divine power. You're not alone. We got you.'*

That number told me, *"Stay grounded. Stand on what you believe. Your prayers been heard, even if the pain still sitting in your chest."*

Then that verse popped in my head:

"Trust in the Lord with all your heart and lean not on your own understanding," Proverbs 3:5.

That hit deep. Like God Himself tapped me on the shoulder and whispered, *"You gon' be alright."*

But still, I had to tell somebody. I couldn't hold all this in. So, I took a deep breath, walked out my room, and headed into the kitchen. My granny was makin' her coffee, her bonnet lopsided and her robe hangin' off one shoulder.

"Granny... I gotta tell you somethin'."

She looked at me over the rim of her cup. "What's wrong, Pooh?"

I swallowed hard. "I lost my virginity."

She damn near choked. "What?! When? Who?! Amber, you better start talkin' right now!"

I told her everythin' about the hospital visit, the burnin,' the itchin,' the trich, the pills, the whole situation with Jabari and how he ghosted me like I was nothin.' Her eyes got big, and her hand covered her chest like I told her somebody died.

"Amber... you need to wear condoms if you gon' be havin' sex. You coulda caught AIDS! Or got pregnant! You are too young for this mess. You hear me? Lord, have mercy on my baby."

I nodded.

"I know... I thought he was different."

She exhaled deep.

"Pooh, I'm proud you held it down this long, but don't move too fast. These lil' dingy-ass niggas just wanna hit and dip. You want somebody who gon' respect you. Who gon' love you for real. Please value yourself, Amber. Protect that body and that heart."

I cried. Not because she was mad... but because she was right. And she still loved me after everythin.'

Later that night, I sat with my diary and wrote every damn word that was sittin' heavy on my chest. The shame, the regret, the tiny hope I had for love that got crushed. I even wrote about how I thought I was pregnant and lowkey felt excited... like maybe that baby would've been someone to love me back.

But God had other plans.

Still, I had to get Jabari outta my system. So, I called Kashae. Yeah, we ain't been hella tight lately, but I had nobody else.

"Damn, Amber... that's wild." Her voice was soft. "Look, I ain't gon' lie. I been on some bullshit, and I know it. It wasn't me tryin' to be fake, it's just me tryna keep my head above water. But I miss you, for real. I don't want no bad blood between us. Can you forgive me?"

I did. Not because I forgot, but because I needed peace. "Yeah, I forgive you."

We talked for a bit, and it felt like a lil' piece of normalcy.

But then... Malachi showed up.

I hadn't seen him since he moved down to the Bay area a while back. I was sweepin' the porch when I saw him walkin' down the street with that same cocky lil' bounce in his step. His locs was longer now—clean, hangin' low, and he had this calm energy about him that made me feel seen.

"Damn... Amber? You still fine as hell." I laughed.

"Boy, shut up. Where you been?"

We talked for a minute. He ain't mention sex. He ain't ask me what I was doin' later. He was just cool. Chill. Grown. He said he was back tryna get his GED and lookin' at trade school. I wasn't expectin' that.

That same night, I brought him up to Granny.

"Who's Malachi?" Granny asked.

"Just an old friend. Nothin' crazy."

She raised her brow. "I hope not. Don't jump from one lil' knucklehead to the next, Amber. Protect yourself. Your peace. Your heart. These lil' boys don't want nothin' but a wet ass and a good lie. Don't be no fool."

"Granny, I ain't. I'm good."

But in my head, I was really startin' to think... maybe I did want more. Maybe I needed to do more for *me*.

So, I made a choice. I went online and looked up the adult education center. The next day, I registered for fall session. Granny clapped when I told her. "Now *that's* what I'm talkin' 'bout, Pooh! That's my baby right there. You ain't lettin' no heartbreak or STD stop you from winnin'!" That's what makes a woman, she keeps goin'!"

And she was right. I ain't let Jabari break me. I wasn't finna let some temporary pain keep me from my permanent purpose. I had three more days of antibiotics, a brand-new chapter startin,' and for the first time in a long time... I felt like maybe, just maybe, I was finally gettin' my power back.

That next mornin', I woke up before the sun. No alarm. No dreams. Just this quiet fire in my chest like I had unfinished business with my own future. That mornin', my stomach was still feelin' a lil off from them antibiotics, but it wasn't like before. The burnin' and the itch, that whole horror story? It was gone now. I was finally feelin' normal again or whatever normal was supposed to feel like after all that.

I had two pills left. Took one with a swig of water, sittin' on the edge of the bed, lookin' out the window like I was waitin' for a sign from the sky or somethin.'

Truth was, my body was healin,' but my mind. My heart? Still wrecked.

Later that day, I took my last pill. Sat it on my tongue, let the water wash it down like I was sayin' goodbye to a chapter of my life I never wanted to live through in the first place. That was it. No more meds. No more symptoms. Just the silence after the storm.

At first, talkin' to Malachi felt like a fresh breeze after a heatwave. We started textin,' chillin' here and there. He had that cool vibe—never pressed, never disrespectful. Real smooth. He ain't come at me like no thirsty dude, and after Jabari, that felt like a blessin.' Malachi had this way of makin' you feel seen. He wasn't too tall, but he had presence. Fade stayed sharp, smile damn near perfect, gold chains layin' right across his collarbone, and he wore 18 carat diamond earrings that made you squint in the sun. He was dressed in Tru Religion or Polo like he was sponsorin' them. He was from the Rollin 60 Crips, but he wasn't no super hardcore thug, just had that quiet danger in him, the kind you didn't question.

Everybody wanted Malachi. And somehow, he wanted *me*.

At least that was what I thought.

We started hangin' more, and little by little, I started noticin' things. He'd slide stuff into conversations real slick. Talkin' bout how he ain't ate all day or how his birthday was comin' up and how bad he wanted them new Jordans that just dropped. I caught it, but I played dumb. Truth was, I wanted to be in love so bad, I let myself believe he was just casually mentionin' things. So, I gave him the money. I did whatever I could to scrape it together just to make him smile.

And he did smile, big, like a lil kid. He kissed my forehead and called me "his rider." That was all I needed to hear. I was fresh outta high school, and yeah, he was younger than me by like a year and a half. He didn't act like it, or maybe I didn't wanna see it.

In the back of my mind, I knew I had to go back and get my diploma. But I was too embarrassed to show my face at the same school everybody thought I graduated from. So, I took time off, told myself I'd figure it out later. I started lookin' at online classes a few times, but my focus was on Malachi. Tryna keep him happy. Tryna prove I was enough.

One day, I walked down to the corner store to clear my head. As soon as I stepped in, I saw a few of the homies from Skyline. We chopped it up for a minute laughin,' clownin' actin' like life wasn't hard. I grabbed some Hot Cheetos and a Sprite, paid for it, and we started walkin' back to the neighborhood together.

We was halfway down the block when this dark, gray Charger rolled up slowly with tinted windows. One window was rolled down just enough for a voice to come out. "Aye, Pnut! You got my money?!"

Everything stopped like time had paused.

The homies stiffened. Hands slid into hoodies. I saw one of 'em grip his waistband just in case. Across the street, them dudes in the car started mean muggin,' lookin' ready for whatever. One of their hands dangled out the window like they wanted to be seen, like they wanted to remind everybody they wasn't playin.'

The tension in the air was thick. Real thick.

I ain't know who Pnut owed, but in that moment, I realized how fast things could flip. One wrong word, one wrong look, and boom. Lives could change. People could die. I clutched my bag of snacks like it could shield me from a bullet.

Then it hit me how reckless I was movin.' Floatin' through life, lettin' these boys distract me from what I needed. Jabari broke my heart. Malachi had me twisted in the head, doin' girlfriend things for a dude who barely gave me boyfriend energy. And now here I was, walkin' with the homies like I wasn't on the edge of throwin' my whole future away.

When I got home, Granny was back in the kitchen, hummin' Yolanda again, swayin' with the beat like she was prayin' with her whole body. She looked at me. "You good, Pooh?"

I nodded, but inside I knew I wasn't.

Not yet.

I went to my room, sat on the bed, and pulled out my phone. I looked up online diploma programs again. This time, I filled out the form. All of it. Hit *submit* before I could second-guess myself. Then I grabbed my diary and wrote.

"*I thought I needed a man to fix me. But maybe I just needed me.*"

CHAPTER NINE

EMOTIONAL ROLLER-COASTER

*Doing too much. Feeling too little.
Searching for something real*

The night Daddy kicked me out, the house felt like it already knew before I did.

The air was heavy and stale like old arguments had been simmerin' in the vents all day. The livin' room lamp threw that yellow light on everythin' on the glass table with the ring from Granny's Pepsi can, on the picture of me in braids from fifth grade, on the faded rug that had seen too many fights and not enough apologies. Even the clock on the wall ticked loudly like it wanted to be heard over us.

I came in quiet. Shoes off by the door. Backpack half-zipped. I knew the rules. I knew the look in his eyes too, the one that said *pick a side, yes sir, or get out.*

He was in his chair, the TV on low, some crime show playin' where everybody lied and the narrator acted like he knew all along. He didn't look at me right away. He was chewin' on the inside of his cheek—jaw tight like the words he wanted were gettin' stuck on their way out.

"Where you been?" His voice cut through the room.

"I told you I had to go see about somethin' after school."

"You 'told me,'" he mocked, turnin' his head slowly, finally pinnin' me down with that stare. "Ain't nobody tell me what they do in *my* house."

I folded my arms across my chest before I could stop myself. My body was tired of bowin.'

"I didn't do nothin' wrong, Daddy."

He stood up like a storm standin' on two legs. "You always got a *reason*. A 'nothin' wrong.' But it's attitude. It's disrespect. It's the way you move."

"The way I move?" I laughed, no humor. "I move how I gotta move. You don't even see me unless you mad."

"Watch your mouth."

"I'm talkin' regular."

"Watch. Your. Mouth."

We stared at each other. The fridge hummed. Somewhere outside, a car alarm chirped twice and stopped. The TV show kept talkin.' The TV show just kept talkin' like life didn't care if you fallin' apart right there. Like life went on even when the scene you livin' in was about to break you open.

He took one step closer. I could smell the faint cologne he wore when he wanted to feel important. He pointed at the hallway with two fingers like a cop who'd been waitin' all day to say it.

"Get your shit."

My stomach dropped.

"For what?"

"Because I'm not talkin' to you no more tonight. I'm done. You wanna be grown? Act grown somewhere else."

"Daddy, stop." My voice cracked on the word *Daddy* like I was six again. "I'm tryin,' okay? I ain't even—"

"Get. Your. Shit."

I wanted him to blink different. To soften. To remember the times he *did* check on me when I was little. The time he bought me the winter coat with the fur hood and told me to zip it all the way up so I wouldn't get sick. I wanted him to be that man for ten seconds.

Instead, he turned his back and sat down like the verdict was printed already.

Somethin' inside me tipped over. I walked down the hall. The carpet fibers chewed at my socks. Every picture on the wall watched me pass the ones Granny forced us to take on Easter, the ones where smiles were arranged like furniture. In my room, I stood at the door and swallowed hard.

The smell in there was me: coconut oil, hair grease, cherry lip gloss, a little laundry detergent from the basket I always forgot to put away. My bed wasn't made. A hoodie was sprawled in the middle of it like a body. A journal was open on the floor with a pen stabbed through the spirals. I should've been safe here. Instead, my hands started movin' before my mind caught up.

I grabbed a black trash bag and stuffed it with T-shirts, jeans, socks balled up the way Granny hated. A pair of sneakers. Two bras. My good scarf. Toothbrush. Edge brush. The small bottle of lotion I kept on my dresser. A picture of me and Granny from the porch, her throwin' up that peace sign, me cheesin' because she was. My journal. The pen. My hands shook so bad, the bag crinkled loud enough to make me flinch.

"Amber." His voice came from the hallway flat, official. "You done?"

I bit down on the inside of my cheek until I tasted metal.

"Almost."

"Don't take nothin' that ain't yours."

"Only thing in here that ain't mine is the bills," I muttered.

"What?"

"Nothin.'" I wiped my eyes with the back of my hand and tied the bag into an ugly knot that looked like a fist that didn't know whether to swing or pray.

I took one more spin in that room; my posters, the chipped mirror with three good angles if I stood just right, the corner where I used to sit cross-legged and wrote when my head felt too loud. The ceilin' had a water stain shaped like a comma. *Pause here,* it seemed to say. *Think.*

I didn't pause. I picked up the bag and walked.

Granny wasn't home; I could feel the empty spot where she would've been, right at the kitchen table, one hand on her cards, cigarette slow burnin,' eyes sharper than the words she'd use to slice open the lie and leave the truth on a napkin. If she was home, this wouldn't be happenin' like this. Or maybe it still would, but at least I'd have a witness who loved me.

I set the bag by the front door and went back for my backpack. Grabbed my charger. Grabbed my little notebook with the bent cover where I wrote the version of me that nobody knew but God. I stood in the doorway to the livin' room and waited for him to look up again.

He didn't. He was starin' at the TV now like the actors had somethin' wise to say.

"I'm gone," I said, voice steady. "You got anything else you wanna say to me?"

He breathed out slow, nostrils flarin.'

"Yeah. Don't be out here embarrassin' my name."

A laugh escaped my throat sideways, cracked and mean. "Your name threw me out."

He turned his head halfway and then stopped himself like even that might be mercy. "Close my door behind you."

I stood there one more second, hopin' the universe would open a trapdoor and sucked me somewhere kinder. It didn't. So, I did what girls like me learned to do early; I swallowed the heat in my chest and made it look like calm. I picked up my bag. I opened the door and walked out.

Outside, the street looked both familiar and hostile. The porch light hummed and threw moth-shadows on the wall. Somewhere a dog barked twice, got bored, quit. The air had that dusty Oakland taste—old sun baked into concrete, car exhaust, somebody grillin' two blocks over. I stepped onto the porch and felt the whole house behind me breathe out like it had been holdin' me in its throat and finally spit me out.

I put the bag down and sat on the top step, elbows on my knees, palms pressed together like prayer and anger were the same shape. My phone screen was spider-cracked, 9% battery blinkin' its threat. My contact list looked longer than my list of people I could actually call.

I scrolled past names that used to mean *home*—old friends who loved to laugh loud but went quiet when life asked for more than jokes, past boys who only called me beautiful when nobody could hear them do it. I hovered over Granny's name even though I knew where she was; over at her sister's playing spades, tellin' somebody the story she always told about how I came out the womb with a frown and a head full of hair. I didn't want to make her choose between me and him from a couch three cities over.

My thumb found Tommy.

I didn't think. I just pressed.

He picked up on the second ring, voice soft but alert the way a person sounded when they know the world liked to sucker punch.

"Amber?" The *r* in my name always sounded safe when he said it. I swallowed.

"Daddy kicked me out."

Silence—two beats, three—then his shoes hit the ground in my ear. "Where you at?"

"At the house."

"Stay there. I'm on the way. Don't go nowhere."

"What if—" I stopped. I didn't want to say *what if he locked the door*. Or *what if he told the neighbors I was crazy?* Or *what if I was crazy?* I just took a deep breath. "Okay."

We hung up. The seconds stretched out thin and mean then folded into minutes. I stared at the street like it owed me an apology. A car rolled past slow; the driver glanced at me like I was furniture on the curb. Across the way, Miss Joan's TV flickered blue behind her curtains. My hands were sweatin'; I wiped them on my jeans and hated how small I felt. Not *little*—small. Two different kinds of hurt. I thought about knockin' on the door. I didn't. Pride and pain held my hands and kept me seated.

Headlights turned the corner and slid up the block like a promise that remembered my name. Tommy's little car pulled to the curb with a whine that said *I'm trying* and *I'm tired* at the same time. He got out fast, hoodie half-zipped, hair flattened on one side, as if he'd jumped up from a nap.

He didn't ask questions at first. He came straight up the steps, saw my face, and somethin' in his shoulders dropped in that way men do when they decided to carry somethin' heavy.

"Come on," he said, voice low like we were hidin' from the night. He grabbed the trash bag, slung it over his shoulder, reached for my backpack and my hand in one motion. His palm was warm, a little rough. It grounded me.

The front door opened behind us. Daddy filled the frame, porch light paintin' a halo that wasn't holy. He didn't step out. Didn't say my name. He just looked past me at Tommy like the problem in his house had a license plate. Tommy nodded once—respectful, not weak.

"Sir."

Daddy's jaw worked.

"You take care of her, you hear?"

It landed weird. A permission that tasted like blame. My cheeks burned. I turned my face to the yard so he wouldn't see me cry.

Tommy didn't answer *yes* or *no*. He just tightened his grip on my hand—a vow he didn't want to put words on.

We walked to the car. I didn't look back. The door clicked shut. The porch light hummed. The house stood quiet and satisfied. My chest felt like a door I couldn't close from the inside.

We pulled off slowly. I watched the block shrink in the side mirror until it was darkness and trees and the memory of me sittin' on a step, pretendin' I knew how to leave and not break.

Tommy turned the radio down low. The kind of volume that allowed you to think but also saved you from drownin' in your thoughts.

"You hungry?" he asked after a block like hunger was a thing you could fix before the rest.

I shrugged, wiped my face with the palm of my hand.

"I don't know."

"I'ma stop at the corner, get you them hot fries you like, and a peach Arizona." His mouth tilted. "Don't argue."

I didn't. The kindness made me want to cry harder. He parked in front of the lil store with the flickering *OPEN* sign and ran in. I stared at the dashboard, and the dust had settled in the vent. My body felt too tall for my skin like grief had stretched me. When he came back, the bag rustled like normal life.

He handed me the chips and the cold can and looked at me long enough to make sure I could meet his eyes. "You with me now. We gon' figure it out."

I cracked the can and let the first cold sip cut through the heat in my throat. "Thank you," I said. My voice sounded small but grateful.

We drove across town. The city looked different from his passenger's seat like the streets were layin' down for us on purpose. We pulled up to his spot, that lil buildin' with the peelin' paint and the gate that squeaked like it wanted to tell all the secrets it had heard. He carried my bag up the stairs and opened his door with that jiggly key that always took a second too long.

Inside, it smelled like laundry soap and something fried, and under that, the quiet scent of a person who lived alone and had learned how to make that not a punishment. The livin' room was simple—couch, low table with a burn ring, TV sittin' crooked on a crate. A lil fan in the corner tried its best. The kitchen was a small, square of tile and hope. The fridge made a rattlin' noise.

He sat the bag down by the couch and turned to me.

"You want the bed. I'll take the couch."

"Tommy, no. I can—"

"Amber." He said my name like a soft instruction. "You had a night. Lay down." I looked at the bedroom door, then back at him.

"Okay."

He disappeared into the kitchen and came back with a chipped mug that was steamy. "Last two tea bags. You get both," he said, tryna smile as though the world wasn't heavy.

I took the mug in both hands. It was too hot, but I held it anyway. "You didn't even ask what happened."

"I don't need to know tonight." He tilted his head. "You safe. That's first."

Something in my chest loosened like a knot realized it didn't have to hold me up anymore. I nodded. "Thank you."

He found me an extra T-shirt and a pair of socks with mismatched stripes. "They clean," he said, suddenly shy.

I laughed through my nose, wiped my face again.

"I didn't think you was gon' give me dirty socks."

"Hey, don't act like you ain't never wore some 'I found these' socks when it's cold."

We laughed a little. He walked me to the bedroom door and leaned his shoulder on the frame, keepin' a respectful distance. "Gimmie your phone. I'll put my charger in. It's faster." I handed it over.

When the door closed, the small room felt like a shelter that remembered me. I sat on the edge of the bed and looked at the ceilin'—no water-stain comma, just clean white with one dead bug stuck in the light cover. My hands trembled slightly. I put the mug on the crate-nightstand and pulled the T-shirt over my head. It fell long on me like a hug.

I crawled under the blanket and felt the mattress dip the way beds did when they were honest about being old. I tucked my knees up and listened to the sounds of his apartment learnin' me—fan whirrin,' fridge murmurin,' the TV in the other room turned to a low-laugh sitcoms. Tommy moved around quietly like he didn't want to scare my peace away.

A tear slid into my ear. I let it. Then another. Then a quiet that wasn't empty, just... done for the day.

From the other side of the door, his voice low, careful.

"You need anything?"

I swallowed. "No. I'm good."

He hesitated. "You are."

The words blanketed the whole room.

I closed my eyes. I thought of Granny's table. I thought of Daddy's door. I thought of the girl I used to be sittin' on the step outside, and the woman I was becomin' slidin' under this blanket, not saved but not alone.

When sleep finally came, it didn't take me by force. It laid down next to me like a promise: *Tomorrow, you still here.* And that was enough to make my fists unclench.

The next morning, light crept through the blinds of Tommy's lil apartment. I opened my eyes slowly, confused for a second until I saw the cracked ceilin' and the fan in the corner barely circulatin' cool air. My chest tightened, remembering everythin'—Daddy's voice, the bag on the porch, Tommy's hand pullin' me from the porch like it was on fire.

The smell of eggs and toast drifted in. I sat up, blanket slidin' off me, and for the first time in a long time, I felt safe. Not fixed, not happy—just safe.

Tommy appeared in the doorway with a chipped plate in his hand and that tired smile he wore like armor.

"Morning," he said. "I made you something."

I laughed, my throat scratchy. "You can cook?"

He shrugged. "I can survive." He set the plate on the crate we were using as a nightstand. Two scrambled eggs, a piece of toast, and one hot link cut in half that was rationed with love.

My chest warmed. "Thank you."

He sat on the edge of the bed, rubbing the back of his neck. "Amber, I know you ain't got nowhere to go right now. I don't want you to feel like… like you a burden or something. You not. You family to me."

Family.

That word wrapped around me like a blanket. I nodded, bitin' my lip to keep from cryin' again.

"I just… I want you to feel like you belong here," he said, voice soft. "Even if I ain't got much."

I reached for his hand. "You already do more than anybody else. Daddy kicked me out, but you—you opened the door."

He squeezed my fingers. "I'll keep opening it. No matter what."

Days turned into weeks, and we built a routine that felt like our own lil world.

The apartment was tiny a living room—one bedroom, a bathroom that always smelled like cheap soap and damp towels but it became home. Tommy worked odd jobs, sometimes at the car wash, sometimes movin' furniture for cash. I did hair in the kitchen, braided kids' hair while their mamas sat on the couch gossipin' and eatin' sunflower seeds.

Money was always tight, but love stretched where dollars couldn't.

We'd sit on the floor at night, countin' change to buy noodles and Kool-Aid. Some days, we laughed so hard about nothin' that my stomach hurt. Other days, the stress sat between us like a third person we couldn't get rid of.

Tommy had his flaws. He didn't always communicate, and sometimes he disappeared for hours without sayin' where he was goin.' But when he came back, he came back to me. That mattered.

I loved him because when Daddy kicked me out, Tommy didn't just give me a place to stay—he gave me *care*. Even when he was strugglin,' he did everythin' to help me.

He made sure I had food before he ate.

He gave me the good pillow when his neck was sore.

He let me dream out loud, even when his own dreams were buried under bills and exhaustion.

But love didn't pay rent. And sometimes, love didn't stop hunger.

One afternoon, my phone buzzed. It was Risha, my old boostin' partner.

"Amber, you tryna make some real money today?" she asked.

I hesitated, glancin' at Tommy. He was asleep on the couch, mouth slightly open, one arm thrown over his face. Rent was due in three days. We had $12 between us.

"Yeah," I said finally. "Where we hittin'?"

We met up near the mall, hoodies on, bags empty but ready. The plan was simple: grab what we could, sell it, pay what needed payin.' It wasn't glamorous, but it kept lights on and food in the fridge.

The adrenaline hit me the moment we walked into the store. My heartbeat synced with the soft pop music playin' overhead. I grabbed shirts, shoes, baby clothes—stuff that would sell fast. My hands moved like they'd been trained for this.

"Two minutes," Risha hissed. We headed toward the exit, casual like we belonged there. But just as we hit the doors, a security guard turned his head.

"Hey! Y'all stop!"

My stomach dropped. We bolted.

We hit the parkin' lot runnin' bags bangin' against our legs. My lungs burned, my legs screamed, but I didn't stop. We dove into Risha's car, breathless and wild. "Go, go, GO!" I yelled.

She peeled out, tires screechin,' laughter bubblin' out of us like we weren't just two girls riskin' everythin' for survival.

By the time we made it back to the apartment, my hands were still shakin.' Tommy looked at me, eyes sharp.

"Amber, what you been doing?"

I froze, then lied through my teeth. "Just… hangin' out with Risha."

He didn't believe me. I could see it in his face. But he didn't push, just sighed and rubbed his temples.

"Be careful," he said. "I can't lose you." His voice cracked on the word *lose*.

As time passed, the pressure started to crack us open.

Tommy hated when I went out hustlin,' but he wasn't bringin' in enough to cover bills alone. Arguments sparked like flint on dry wood.

"You out there doing God knows what," he yelled one night, pacin' the tiny livin' room. "What if you get caught? What if you don't come home?"

"What if we don't eat?" I shot back. "You think I *like* this? I'm doin' what I gotta do because nobody else will!"

His eyes glistened.

"Amber, I just want you safe."

I softened for a second, but pride kept my mouth hard.

"Safe don't keep the lights on."

We stood there, breathin' heavy; two people who loved each other, but didn't know how to fight *for* each other instead of against each other.

Weeks later, my body felt different.

Nausea. Sore breasts. A heaviness I couldn't explain.

I bought a pregnancy test and stared at it in the bathroom, heart poundin.'

Two pink lines.

Pregnant.

I slid down the wall, the cold tile pressin' against my back. Memories flooded me—Daddy's harsh words, Granny's warm hands, the way Tommy had carried me out of my father's house that night.

This baby would change everythin.'

I just didn't know if it would save us or break us.

I sat there on the bathroom floor, the pregnancy test clutched so tight in my hand, it left little marks on my skin.

The whole world felt like it was spinnin'—the hum of the fridge, the distant sound of traffic outside, even my own heartbeat felt too loud.

Tommy was in the livin' room, playin' the same beat-up PlayStation he always played when he was stressed. The sound of gunshots and fake sirens from the game bled into the silence of the apartment.

I wiped my face with the back of my hand and forced myself to stand up. My legs felt like they were made of bricks.

When I stepped out of the bathroom, he looked up at me, controller in his hand, brow furrowed.

"You good?" he asked, his voice cautious. "You look… pale."

"I need to talk to you." I swallowed hard, tryna steady my breathing.

The way I said it must've told him everythin' because his face dropped instantly.

He set the controller down slow like he already knew this conversation was about to change us.

"Amber... what's wrong?"

"I'm pregnant." I held up the test, my hand tremblin.'

I remember starin' at that pregnancy test for what felt like forever, my hands shakin,' my chest hot. Two lines. Clear as day. November 2012.

I sat there quietly, tryna hear my own heartbeat over the noise in my head. I was twenty-one and halfway ready for nothin.'

"Damn, for real? That's crazy... but I'm happy though." I watched his face to see if the words matched the feelin.' They didn't. He hugged me, but it felt like he was huggin' a problem he didn't know how to fix yet.

That night, I laid in his lap and said, "We really 'bout to be parents."

"Yeah, it's time to grow up," he said. But deep down, I already knew I was the only one who would.

When I told my daddy, I was nervous like a teenager caught sneakin' in late, but he took it better than I thought. He looked at me, sighed, and said, "Well, it is what it is now. You gon' be a good mama. Just stay focused."

My family was cool about it. Nobody yelled. Nobody disowned me. My aunties said congratulations. My granny rubbed my stomach and said, "Babies bring blessings, even when they come early."

Tommy's family, though? Whole different story.

His mama side-eyed me from day one like I stole her son instead of carryin' his child.

They'd whisper and say things like, "She trappin' him," or "He too young to be tied down."

It stung, but I stayed quiet. I was too busy tryna protect what was growin' inside me. A few months in, I started feelin' weird pressure low in my stomach. At first, I thought it was normal, but somethin' didn't feel right.

When I went to my OB/GYN, she checked me, looked serious, and said, "Your cervix is shortening faster than we'd like. You have what's called an incompetent cervix."

My heart dropped.

"Incompetent?" The word itself sounded like an insult. I sat up on that cold table, paper stickin' to my thighs, and asked, "So what does that mean for my baby?"

"It means we need to place a cerclage. Basically, a stitch to help your body hold the pregnancy," she said.

I didn't know what a cerclage was, but I knew it sounded like somethin' that could change everything.

They immediately referred me to a high-risk pregnancy specialist.

The next week, I was sittin' in another doctor's office with bright lights and machines everywhere. They slid that vaginal scope in and started explainin' everythin' how they'd go in through my cervix, sew it shut with a strong thread, and pray my body cooperated.

I nodded, pretendin' I was calm, but inside I was screamin.'

The day of the cerclage, I remember puttin' on that thin hospital gown, tyin' it behind my neck, and tryna not to cry.

Tommy sat in the corner on his phone, scrollin' like we wasn't about to do surgery on the life we made.

I wanted to tell him I was scared, but pride got in the way.

The nurse came in with that kind smile that didn't reach the eyes. She said, "You'll feel some pressure."

Pressure turned into pain.

I gripped the edge of that bed so tight, my knuckles turned white. Tears came without askin' for permission.

They had my legs up, lights blindin,' machines beepin,' and I swear it felt like my whole soul was on that table.

I cried the whole way through. Not loud. Just the kind of cryin' that choked you up silent.

It hurt so bad like my body was fightin' to keep a promise it didn't make.

When it was over, I was sore and dizzy. They wheeled me back to recovery and said, "You did great."

I didn't feel great. I felt broken but determined.

Tommy walked over and asked, "You good?"

"I will be," I said. That was the truth. I *would* be, eventually. Just not that day.

At home, I moved slow. Every step reminded me I was stitched up, fragile, responsible for two lives—mine and hers.

My mama cooked for me. My family checked in.

Tommy came around when he felt like it. I learned early that love didn't keep appointments. Still, every night I laid my hand on my belly and whispered, "We gon' make it, baby. You hear me? We gon' make it."

And she must've heard me 'cause she stayed.

Through every ache, every tear, every lonely night—she stayed. Me and Tommy stayed together on and off for about three years.

Love was heavy back then; the kind you dragged instead of carried.

We'd argue one day and be fine the next, but the fine never lasted long.

He had this habit of leavin' when things got real.

If we fought, he'd disappear for days at his mama's house like I was the problem that needed space instead of a woman who needed help.

Sometimes, I'd wake up and he'd be gone—no text, no call.

I'd be sittin' there, big belly, tryna figure out how to make it through another day alone.

But I still got up.

Caught that bus to school.

Caught another one to work.

Sometimes, I'd walk half a mile just to save transfer fare. Heat burnin' my skin, cold bitin' my fingers didn't matter. I was carryin' a baby and a dream, and neither one was light.

When I came home, I'd find his friends posted up, eatin' my food like they paid bills.

His cousins crashed on the floor, shoes kicked off, mouths runnin,' music loud.

One time, I came home and found somebody wearin' my hoodie like it was theirs. Another day, I noticed little things missin'—earrings, cash, food.

They'd laugh and say, "Girl, chill, you trippin.'"

But I wasn't. I was survivin' in chaos that didn't belong to me.

I tried to talk to Tommy about it.

"Why your people always in our business? Why they always here?" I asked him.

"That's my family. They ain't hurtin' nobody." He'd shrug and say.

But they *were*.

They was stealin' my peace one visit at a time.

They whispered about me in the kitchen, asked me questions bein' nosey, treated me like an outsider in my own space.

One day I told him, "You gotta choose. You gon' build with me or you gon' keep lettin' them run through our house like a motel."

"You always actin' like it's me versus them." He'd laugh and say.

"That's because it is," I would say.

He got quiet then grabbed his keys and left again.

And that was the rhythm—fight, leave, return, repeat.

When he was gone, I'd sit on the couch with my feet swollen, rubbin' cocoa butter on my belly, whisperin' to the baby. "It's okay, Mama got you. We gon' be good, with or without him."

Those were the nights I learned independence the hard way.

The nights I cried into my pillow so I wouldn't wake the baby kickin' inside me.

The nights I realized I was lovin' somebody who only showed up halfway.

I started noticin' little things, the freedom in bein' alone. The quiet after the noise left.

When I'd come home to no one, I could breathe again.

No more arguments, no more freeloaders, no more fake love.

Just me, my baby, and the sound of my heartbeat g'tting' stronger.

But somehow, I always let him back.

Not because I believed he'd change, but because I didn't know how to stop hopin.'

He'd come home with that soft voice. "I'm sorry, I was trippin.' You know I love you."

And I'd melt because the truth was, I did love him.

But love didn't fix lazy. Love didn't fix loyalty to the wrong people.

By the time I was eight months pregnant, I knew he wasn't comin' home for good.

I'd accepted that his family came first, and I came last.

And it hurt because I wasn't built to give up on people, even when they already gave up on me.

So, I just stopped expectin.'

Stopped askin' him to stay.

Stopped beggin' him to grow.

I focused on finishin' school, savin' money, and preparin' for my baby.

Some nights, I'd catch the last bus home, sit by the window, and watch the city lights blur by. My hands rested on my belly, and I'd whisper to my baby. "We gon' make it, baby. One day, we gon' have peace. Not this kind, the real kind."

And deep down, I knew I was tellin' the truth.

July 20th, 2013. That morning, the sun came up slow like it was scared to start the day. I was already in pain; that dull, deep ache that made you want to crawl out your own skin. My belly felt heavy, tight, like it had outgrown me.

At the hospital, the nurse checked my vitals and said my blood pressure was creepin.' "We're going to take her today," she told me.

I nodded, numb. The doctor said C-section, and all I could think was, *Lord, please let my baby be okay.*

They wheeled me into that freezin' operating room. The lights were too bright, too white, no comfort in sight.

Fail to See

I laid there—shakin,' starin' up at the ceilin' tiles while they prepped me.

Tommy was supposed to be there, and he was, but his spirit wasn't. He stood to the side quietly like he was watchin' someone else's life happen.

When the anesthesia kicked in, everythin' felt like slow motion. I could hear the clinkin' of instruments, smelled the sterilizer, felt pressure deep in my stomach.

The doctor said, "You're going to feel some tugging."

Tuggin' wasn't the word. It felt like they were pullin' my whole world into existence.

And then a cry.

Small, high, and shaky.

They lifted her up and said, "It's a girl."

Five pounds, ten ounces. Tiny and beautiful like she'd been painted by angels intentionally.

They placed her near me, and I swear time stopped. I whispered, "Hi, baby. It's me. I got you."

After the surgery, I expected peace, but peace didn't come easy.

A few hours later, they said she wasn't eatin' enough.

Her little lips barely latched, her body tremblin' like she was fightin' air itself.

Then the nurse said her temperature dropped, she'd gotten cold.

Next thing I knew, they were rollin' her away in that clear plastic crib, wires everywhere, nurses talkin' fast. "We're taking her to the NICU."

Those words hit me harder than the surgery.

I couldn't move, stitches tight, body still numb from the waist down. All I could do was cry and pray under my breath. "God, please keep her warm. Please don't take her."

My granny was there. She held my hand and said, "Baby, she gon' be fine. God got her."

My daddy came too—quiet and steady—standin' at the end of my bed like a soldier guardin' his child and grandchild at once.

A few of my cousins showed up, bringin' that loud love I didn't even realize I needed.

Even Tommy's family came—his mama, aunts, cousins—all standin' around actin' concerned. I appreciated it, but it felt weird. The same ones who side-eyed me before were suddenly whisperin' prayers now. I let them. The moment wasn't about pride; it was about survival.

The NICU was its own world.

Cold air, beepin' monitors, the smell of sanitizer everywhere.

I sat in that wheelchair, starin' at her through the incubator. My tiny girl wrapped in tubes and wires, little chest risin' slow like she was learnin' how to breathe all over again.

Five pounds had dropped to five ounces.

I whispered through the glass, "Come on, baby. Eat for mama. You stronger than they know."

Her skin looked too soft for this world.

But even then, I could see the fight in her that spark that said, *I ain't done yet.*

Every few hours, I'd roll down there—scar burnin,' stomach sore, but I didn't care. I'd pump milk even when nothin' came out, just prayin' something in me could reach her.

I'd sit for hours talkin' to her like she could hear me. "You came from strength, baby girl. Don't let go now."

Days passed.

Her weight started creepin' back up.

5 pounds, 2 ounces.

5 pounds, 4 ounces.

The nurse said, "She's doing better."

And when they finally let me hold her again, the wires were gone and the warmth was back in her skin. I cried so hard; the nurse cried, too.

My granny kissed her forehead and said, "Told you she was gon' be alright."

Daddy nodded, quiet but proud.

Tommy just stood there, hands in his pockets, eyes low. I didn't even need words to know his part in this story was fadin.'

That night in the hospital room, I laid her on my chest; her little heartbeat against mine.

The world outside could've ended and I wouldn't have noticed.

I whispered, "You five pounds of faith, and you changed everything. I thought I was strong before, but now I know."

And for the first time since that test turned positive, I felt peace. Not because everythin' was fixed, but because we made it. That night, Tommy and I was laid in the bed, our hands entwined over my stomach.

The TV flickered in the background, but we weren't really watchin' it.

"We gonna be okay," he whispered. "I'll make sure of it."

I wanted to believe him.

I wanted to believe that love would be enough to keep us whole.

But as I stared at the ceilin,' I realized somethin.'

Whether Tommy stayed or left, whether my daddy ever softened, whether the streets ever gave me peace, this baby was mine.

And I would never let the world break them the way it tried to break me.

"I don't know what tomorrow looks like," I wrote, my pen tremblin.' *"But tonight, I promise my baby this: we will rise."*

CHAPTER TEN

MOTHERHOOD & MAYHEM

The joy, the pressure, the fight to protect and provide

After bein' in the hospital with Niaomy for a week, she was finally cleared to go home. The first night at home was pure chaos.

I thought the hard part was over after givin' birth, but nobody told me that labor was just the beginnin' of a whole new battlefield.

My body was sore in places I didn't even know could hurt. My arms ached from holdin' her. My back throbbed from hours of labor. Every step felt like I was walkin' on broken glass. But there was no time to think about any of that because this tiny human was dependin' on me.

She cried and cried like her little lungs were on fire, and nothin' calmed her down.

I tried rockin' her, feedin' her, swaddlin' her tight like the nurse had shown me.

Nothin' worked for long.

Tommy hovered nearby, lookin' just as lost as I felt. He tried, but the way he held her was awkward, his nerves showed. I couldn't blame him; neither of us had ever done this before. We were two young adults raisin' a kid, figurin' it out in real-time.

By sunrise, I was a zombie. My eyes burned, my head pounded, and my shirt was damp from milk leakin' through the fabric.

I sat on the edge of the bed, cradlin' my daughter while tears streamed down my face silently. Not because I regretted her—never that—but because the weight of it all was crushin' me.

"Baby, let me take her for a while," Tommy said gently, reachin' for her.

I hesitated then handed her over. Watchin' him walk back and forth in the dim light, whisperin' to her, I felt a mix of gratitude and loneliness.

He was here physically, but emotionally? I wasn't sure where he stood yet.

Granny came by later that day, her soft hands smellin' like lotion and peppermint candy.

She scooped up her great-grandbaby like she'd been waitin' her whole life for this moment.

"Look at her, Pooh," Granny said, her eyes glistenin.' "She perfect. Just like you were when you was born."

I leaned into her hug, lettin' some of my tension melt away. Granny had a way of makin' even the hardest moments feel a little lighter.

"Granny, I'm so tired," I confessed, my voice crackin.' "I don't know if I'm doing this right."

She cupped my face in her hands. "Baby, ain't no perfect way to do this. You just love her the best you can, and that's enough."

Her words hit deep, but part of me still didn't believe them.

I'd grown up feelin' unloved, unwanted at times. The idea of givin' my baby the kind of consistent love I never had felt both healin' and terrifyin.'

Weeks passed, and life settled into a messy, exhaustin' rhythm.

Mornings started with diaper changes and warm bottles, the smell of formula lingerin' in the air. I'd balance her on one hip while tryna fold laundry or answer texts with my free hand.

I didn't have time to think about myself. Showers were a luxury. Meals were whatever I could grab one-handed between feedings. Sleep was somethin' I only got in thirty-minute bursts.

But I refused to let motherhood stop my grind.

I enrolled in community college, determined to build a better future for both of us. My classes were durin' the day, and at night, I worked double shifts first at a burger joint off E. 14th, then at a call center on Hegenberger. My feet stayed swollen, my back screamed at me, but I kept going.

Some nights, Granny watched the baby. When she couldn't, Tommy stepped in.

I hated dependin' on him so much, but I didn't have a choice. This wasn't just my dream anymore; it was ours.

The cracks started to show once the sleepless nights piled up and money ran low.

"Amber, you always at work or school," Tommy snapped one night, pacin' the livin' room. "When you even gon' have time for us?"

I sat down the bottle I was washin' and glared at him. "For *us*? I'm doin' this for our daughter, Tommy. For you. For me. You think I *like* runnin' myself into the ground?"

He threw his hands up. "I'm here too, you know. I'm tryin.'"

"Tryin' ain't enough," I shot back, my voice tremblin.' "She deserves more than tryin.'"

The fight spiraled until Granny walked in, her presence cuttin' through the tension like a knife.

"Y'all need to get it together," she said sharply, her gaze movin' between us. "This baby don't need chaos. She needs love."

We both went quiet, guilt heavy in the air.

Despite the fights, despite the exhaustion, I kept pushin' forward.

There were moments—small, fleetin' ones—that reminded me why I fought so hard.

Like when my daughter wrapped her tiny hand around my finger and wouldn't let go.

Or when Granny sang her old gospel hymns while rockin' her to sleep, her voice fillin' the room with warmth.

These were the moments I clung to when everythin' else felt like it was fallin' apart.

But love didn't pay bills.

And no matter how hard I worked, there were days when I'd open the fridge and saw nothin' but a carton of eggs and a half-empty bottle of juice.

That was when the streets started whisperin' to me again.

The hustle was always there, waitin,' promisin' quick money.

I tried to ignore it, to stay clean for my baby's sake, but survival didn't care about good intentions.

One night, after puttin' my daughter to bed, I sat at the kitchen table starin' at a shut-off notice from PG&E. The weight of it crushed me. I thought about Granny's words, about breakin' cycles… but right then, all I could think about was keepin' the lights on.

I picked up my phone and sent a single text to Risha.

You still running?

Her reply came fast.

Always.

Risha met me outside the corner store; her hoodie pulled low, eyes dartin' like we was up to no good because we were.

The streets had a certain smell at night: weed, fried food, and somethin' unspoken like danger mixed with desperation.

"You ready, Amber?" she asked, tossin' me a pair of black gloves.

I caught them without a word. My heart was poundin,' but I didn't let it show. This wasn't about thrill-seekin'; this was survival.

The first job back felt like muscle memory.

Slip in, grab what we needed, get out before anyone caught on.

My stomach twisted the whole time, not from fear but from the weight of knowin' why I was there.

Every can of formula, every pack of diapers, every dollar in my pocket had my daughter's name on it.

When we got back to my place, I stashed the goods under the bed and sat on the floor, head in my hands.

I could hear my baby breathin' softly from her crib. That sound was the only thing that kept me from breakin' completely.

As my hustle picked up, Tommy started slippin.'

He'd disappear for hours, sometimes days, comin' back smellin' like smoke and cheap cologne.

"Where you been?" I asked one night, arms crossed, baby on my hip.

"Out handling business," he said, not meetin' my eyes.

"Business, huh? The kind that don't pay bills?"

He glared at me. "You always got somethin' to say."

"Because I'm the one holdin' everything together, Tommy! Me and this baby! While you out here playin' like you still single." The fight escalated until Granny had to step in, baby cryin' in the background.

"That's enough!" she yelled, her voice tremblin' but firm. "This house don't need no more yellin.' Y'all either fix it or leave it."

We both went quiet, but nothin' was really fixed.

The distance between us grew wider every day.

Through it all, Granny stayed solid.

She'd rock the baby and hum those old gospel songs, her voice like a balm on an open wound.

"Pooh, you stronger than you think," she'd tell me, lookin' me dead in the eyes. "You came from strong women. You just gotta keep walkin.'"

Sometimes I'd sit beside her and just cry, lettin' her words sink into the cracks the world had left in me.

Granny didn't have much. No fancy car, no big house, just love and wisdom. But that was worth more than gold.

One night, Tommy came home late again. I'd been up all night with the baby, tryna soothe her fever, my eyes red and swollen from exhaustion.

"Tommy, where the hell you been?" I demanded.

"Out." He shrugged, slippin' off his shoes like it was nothin.'

"Out where? You got a daughter here who needed you!"

"She got you," he said coldly. "Ain't like she need both of us." My chest tightened.

"That's where you wrong. She needs a father, Tommy. She needs to see what real love looks like."

He scoffed.

"Real love don't pay bills."

That was it.

The line I couldn't cross back from. "Get out," I said, my voice shakin' but firm.

"What?"

"Get. Out."

Tommy stared at me for a moment like he didn't recognize the woman standin' in front of him.

Then he grabbed his bag and walked out, slammin' the door so hard it rattled the windows.

I sank to the floor, clutchin' my baby to my chest, whisperin' over and over, "It's just me and you now. Just me and you."

A few weeks later, my cousin, Risha, came by.

She looked nervous, her hands fidgetin' with the hem of her hoodie.

"What's up, girl?" I asked, handin' her a soda. She sat down slowly.

"Amber… I'm pregnant." The words hung in the air like a heavy fog. I stared at her, my mind racin.'

"Damn, Risha. You sure?" She nodded, tears fillin' her eyes.

"Yeah. Took three tests."

I hugged her tight, memories of my own pregnancy flooded back.

"I know you scared," I said softly. "But you ain't alone. We gon' figure this out together."

Her news hit me hard because it mirrored my own journey.

It reminded me how easy it was for cycles to repeat if nobody broke them.

Days blurred into nights, and nights into endless to-do lists.

School. Work. Hustle. Baby.

I'd collapse into bed at dawn, only to be woken up an hour later by a hungry cry.

Sometimes I'd stare at the ceilin' and wonder if I was strong enough to keep going.

But every time my daughter smiled, every time she reached for me, I knew I couldn't quit.

I had to show her a different life even if it killed me in the process.

The hustle wasn't free.

With every job, the risks grew higher.

One night, things went left. Way left.

Me and Risha had just hit a spot when a security guard came out of nowhere, yellin' for us to stop. My heart pounded as we ran, our feet slappin' the pavement, breath ragged. We barely made it into the car, laughin' and cryin' at the same time.

"That was too close," Risha gasped, clutchin' her chest. I stared out the window, shakin.'

"We can't keep doin' this. One day, we ain't gon' get away." But deep down, I knew I wasn't ready to let go either. The streets had their hooks in me too deep.

One night, after puttin' my baby to bed, I sat at the kitchen table with my journal.

The pages were worn, stained with tears and ink.

I wrote:

"Tonight, I feel like I'm drownin.' But tomorrow, I'll swim. I have to. Because my daughter needs to see a woman who refused to sink."

I closed the journal, wiped my eyes, and whispered to myself, "Tomorrow starts a new fight."

And with that, I set the stage for everythin' to come the battles, the healin,' and the slow, painful process of breakin' free.

CHAPTER ELEVEN

LETTING GO TO GROW

Moving on, moving out, and learning how to walk away.

The night Tommy left, the air in the room felt colder than it had ever been.

The slam of the door rattled the walls, but what really broke me was the silence that followed.

It wasn't just him walkin' out, it was everything: every hope I had for a family, every late-night dream about stability, every prayer whispered into the dark when I thought maybe, just maybe, we could make it work.

I sat on the floor, my back against the couch, holdin' my baby girl so tight; I was scared I might hurt her. She was cryin,' but it was soft, tired cries, as though she already picked up on my heartbreak. I rocked her back and forth, my tears fallin' into her soft curls. "It's just me and you now," I whispered. "Just me and you."

For the first time since she was born, the weight of single motherhood settled on my chest. It felt like a boulder. There was no backup plan. No one to swoop in and save me. Tommy was gone. Granny was still my rock, but she couldn't be everything.

It was just me.

Me against the world.

I decided to pick up another journal this time—one with a lock to assure nobody could ever get inside my thoughts again. No matter what I said, I could never escape from writin'; it was somethin' I loved doin' like second nature to me. I had been havin' some different emotions and men had been the least thing from my mind, all they did was hurt me…I wanted somethin' gentle, more like me with an emotional attachment. Lately, I'd been starin' at women more than usual. I knew it was against my religion, but it was my feelings and they were valid. I wanted to try somethin' different. I wanted to know what it felt like to be loved by a woman…

The next morning, I woke up to the sound of my baby fussin' in her crib.

My whole body ached, eyes were swollen from cryin,' breasts were sore, back was stiff, but I pushed myself up because there was no one else to do it.

I changed her diaper, kissed her forehead, and then sat in the kitchen starin' at a half-empty box of cereal and a light bill with "FINAL NOTICE" stamped in red across the top.

Tears welled up again, but this time I swallowed them down.

"No time to cry, Amber," I told myself. "Get up and figure it out."

The fridge was almost bare, just a carton of eggs and some leftover spaghetti from two nights ago. I made a mental list: diapers, formula, groceries, and bus fare to get to work and back.

The list was overwhelmin,' and my courage felt too small against it. The list towered over me, darin' my courage to measure up.

But I still packed up my baby, strapped her into her car seat, and headed out.

Everywhere we went, people stared with pity or judgment. I kept my head high even though I felt like collapsin' on the inside.

As I walked down the block toward the bus stop, I heard Granny's voice in my head.

"Pooh, you stronger than you think. You came from strong women. Don't let this world break you."

Those words carried me.

Every step I took, every bag I lugged home, every shift I worked with achin' feet, it was done with her voice echoin' in my mind.

Granny couldn't be there every day, but she showed up for me and my baby in ways no one else could.

She'd rock her great-grandbaby to sleep, hummin' old gospel songs while I sat in the corner and finally exhaled. For those moments, I felt safe. Seen.

The bills didn't stop comin' just because my heart was broken.

Rent was due.

Lights were about to be cut off.

Diapers weren't free.

And that was when the streets started whisperin' to me again.

I had promised myself I was done with all that boostin,' hustlin,' runnin' with people who didn't have anything to lose.

But when you were faced with your baby goin' hungry, all those promises started to crumble.

One night, I sat at the kitchen table, the baby finally asleep, starin' at a stack of shut-off notices.

My chest felt tight.

I thought about Tommy, about how he left me to handle it all.

I thought about my daddy the way he talked about me to the family and the shit he say to my face, still findin' ways to control me with his words. I thought about Granny bein' stretched thin, tryna hold our whole family together.

And then I thought about my baby girl.

Her smile. Her soft little hands reachin' for me.

I couldn't let her down.

I picked up my phone and sent one text to Risha.

You still running?

Her reply came back almost instantly.

Always.

The night air felt different when you were about to cross a line you swore you'd never cross again.

Me and Risha met up outside a corner store—hoodies up, gloves tucked in our pockets.

"You ready?" she asked, eyes scannin' the street like a hawk.

I nodded, even though my heart was poundin' so loud it felt like everyone could hear it.

This wasn't excitement, it was desperation.

We slipped inside quick, smooth, grabbin' what we needed with precision.

Formula, baby wipes, a few other essentials.

My hands were steady, but inside I was shakin.'

We got out clean—no alarms, no yellin,' just silence and heavy breathin' as we sped away.

Back at my place, I stashed everythin' under the bed and sat on the floor, clutchin' my knees.

The baby was asleep, her soft breathin' filling the room.

"I did what I had to do for you," I whispered. "I'll always do what I have to do."

But deep down, guilt gnawed at me. I knew this road didn't have a happy endin.' That night, after Risha left, I pulled out my journal.

"Tonight, I went back to the streets. Not because I wanted to, but because survival don't give a damn about morals. My baby won't remember these days, but I will. I just pray one day she understands why I did what I did."

I closed the journal and sat in the dark, rockin' slowly, tears streamin' down my face. The room was heavy, but eventually the silence pushed me back into the rhythm of life. Days blurred together, nothin' dramatic, just one moment foldin' into the next.

That night, Risha convinced me to come out for a little while just to breathe. I wanted to argue, but deep down, she was right. I hadn't been Amber in a long time. I'd been Mama. Provider. Protector. Warrior… everything but me. So, I went.

We pulled up to a small apartment on the east side. The bass from the music was thumpin' so loud, it rattled the windows. Laughter and voices spilled into the hallway as the door swung open, smoke driftin' out like a warnin.' Inside, the air was thick with weed, sweat, and cheap liquor. People were everywhere posted up on couches, playin' spades at the table, and dancin' in the kitchen. I stayed close to Risha, tryna blend in. My eyes scanned the room, always on alert. That was when I saw him. He wasn't the loudest in the room or the flashiest.

He was just leanin' against the wall, quiet, watchin' everything like he was takin' mental notes.

Tall, smooth brown skin, hair cut close with a clean fade, gold chain glintin' under the dim lights.

Our eyes met for half a second, and somethin' in his stare felt… steady.

Not like he was tryna figure out how to use me, but like he was tryna figure out how to understand me.

Later, when the crowd shifted and Risha went to grab drinks, he slid over next to me.

"You don't look like you wanna be here," he said, voice low and calm.

I smirked. "I don't. I'd rather be home with my baby."

"You got a kid?"

"Yeah," I said, my tone guarded. "My whole world." He nodded with respect instead of judgment.

"Ain't nothin' wrong with that. Most people don't even take care of they own."

The conversation flowed easily after that.

He wasn't tryin' too hard, and he didn't come with slick lines like other dudes.

We talked about random stuff—music, childhood memories, dumb things people did when they were bored.

It was… normal.

And for me, normal felt like luxury.

Over the next few weeks, Malachi kept showin' up consistently. He'd check on me through text.

You good today?

Need anything for the baby?

Don't forget to eat.

Nobody ever asked me that last one.

People were quick to ask me for things, quick to need me but not many cared if I had eaten, if I was okay, if I was more than just a provider.

Malachi made me laugh.

Like really laugh that deep, belly laugh I hadn't felt in a long time.

He'd tell me stupid jokes, tease me about my old-school music playlists, and listened when I vented about school, work, or my daddy.

But more than that, he made me feel seen.

The problem wasn't Malachi.

The problem was me or maybe it was the trauma livin' inside me like a squatter who refused to leave. I was so used to chaos that calm felt suspicious. When Malachi didn't raise his voice or disappear for days like Tommy, I'd start overthinkin.'

Is he hiding something?

Is this real or is he just better at lying?

Some nights, I'd lay awake starin' at the ceilin,' my baby curled beside me, Malachi's text glowin' on my phone's screen.

My heart wanted to trust him, but my mind was a battlefield of memories.

Kash's betrayal.

Tommy walkin' out.

My new emotions about goin' to the otha side....

My daddy's sharp words cuttin' me down even when he wasn't there.

I started journalin' more during this time, tryna untangle my thoughts.

"Why do I keep letting people in who might leave? Why do I keep loving like my heart ain't been broken before? Maybe because if I stop loving, I'll disappear completely."

One night, everything came to a head.

I had been runnin' all day with work, school, and babysitters fallin' through. When I finally got home, Malachi was waitin' on the steps.

He stood up when he saw me, hands in his pockets, lookin' nervous. "We need to talk," he said.

My chest tightened. Those four words always meant trouble.

We went inside, and he told me some of his own struggles, his family drama, how he'd been tryna help his younger brother stay out of trouble, and how he was worried about makin' ends meet.

It wasn't an excuse, just honesty.

For once, I saw him as someone who was fightin' his own battles, not someone who would hurt me.

That night, after he left, I sat at the edge of my bed watchin' my daughter sleep.

I thought about the cycles I'd been stuck in—love, betrayal, survival.

I thought about Granny and the lessons she tried to teach me.

I thought about the little girl inside me who never got to feel safe, and how she still lived in my chest, cryin' out for protection.

I realized somethin' important: I couldn't just keep survivin.' I had to start healin.'

And healin' didn't mean cuttin' everyone off or pretendin' like I didn't need love them.

It meant learnin' to love myself enough to stop settlin' for less.

It was a rainy night, the kind where the whole city felt like it was holdin' its breath.

I had just dropped my daughter off at Granny's for the night. My plan was simple: hit a quick run with Risha, grab what we needed, and get back before sunrise.

"Amber, you sure you good?" Granny asked as I buckled up my baby girl. I forced a smile.

"Yeah, Ma. I'll be back before she wakes up."

But inside, my nerves were shot. Every run was a gamble, and I hated the thought of leavin' my baby to dance with danger.

Me and Risha rolled through the backstreets, music low, windows cracked.

The rain hit the windshield in sheets, blurrin' streetlights into glowin' streaks.

"You ready?" she asked, her voice tight.

I nodded, even though my stomach twisted.

I didn't want to be there, but I couldn't see another way out.

We made it inside—smooth and silent.

But just as we were headin' for the door, a voice boomed behind us. "Hey! What the hell y'all doing?!"

Time froze.

Then chaos exploded.

Risha dropped the bag and bolted.

I followed, heart poundin' so hard, it drowned out the sound of my feet.

We hit the alley, rain soakin' us, our breaths ragged and loud.

I could hear heavy footsteps behind us, gettin' closer. "Amber, go left!" Risha screamed.

We split up, and I dove behind a dumpster, crouchin' low, shakin' so bad, I thought my teeth would shatter.

I stayed there until the footsteps faded and the world went quiet again except for the rain.

When I finally stumbled out, soaked and breathless, Risha was gone.

I walked home that night with nothin' but regret weighin' me down.

My shoes squished with every step, my hoodie clung to my skin, and my soul felt like it was unravelin.'

When I got to Granny's, she was asleep in her chair with my baby curled on her chest.

The sight stopped me in my tracks.

I stood in the doorway, drippin' rainwater, starin' at them like they were the last two people on earth.

And in that moment, it hit me.

I couldn't keep doin' this.

I couldn't keep riskin' my life for scraps while my baby slept, unaware of how close her mama came to not comin' home.

I couldn't keep repeatin' cycles that would swallow us whole.

The next day, Malachi came by. I didn't even try to play strong. I collapsed into his arms, sobbin,' every muscle in my body tremblin' from the night before.

He didn't ask questions right away. He just held me, rockin' slightly, his voice low and steady.

"You safe now. I got you." And for a brief moment, I let myself believe it.

Later that night, after everyone was asleep, I sat alone by the window, lookin' out at the rain-slick streets. I opened my journal and wrote.

"I almost lost myself tonight. I almost lost everything. But God gave me another chance. I don't know how many more chances I got left, but I'm done gamblin' with my life. For her. For me. For all the women in my family who never got free."

I closed the journal, wiped my face, and whispered into the dark. "This cycle ends with me."

CHAPTER TWELVE

HEALING AIN'T PRETTY BUT IT'S NECESSARY

Closing doors that nearly destroyed me

The mornings hit different now. It wasn't just about me anymore. It was about her—the tiny human who depended on me to show up—no matter how empty I felt inside.

The first thing I always heard was her soft little sounds, those coos and hums babies made when they were still half-asleep, halfway between a dream and wakin' up. Sometimes she'd kick the crib's rail with her little socked feet like she was tryna tell me, *"Mama, it's time. We got stuff to do."*

I'd sit up slowly, my body stiff and sore, my back achin' like an old woman's.

Sleep was a luxury I rarely had anymore. Between late-night feedings, work, and school assignments, I averaged maybe three or four hours of sleep on a good night. My eyes felt heavy every morning, but when I looked over and saw her starin' back at me with those big, trustin' eyes, it gave me just enough fuel to keep goin.'

"Good morning, baby girl," I'd whisper, voice scratchy from sleep.

She'd smile wide, gums showin' like the whole world wasn't so bad after all.

I had a system. A routine that kept me from unravelin' completely.

I warmed a washcloth, cleaned her little face and hands, lotioned her skin so she smelled like baby powder and sunshine. I changed her diaper, wrestled her into a fresh onesie while she wiggled and giggled like it was a game.

Then I'd put on some soft music, old R&B, somethin' smooth and we'd sway together quietly. She didn't know it, but those mornings kept me alive as much as they kept her cared for.

I'd sit her in the highchair with some mashed bananas while I threw together oatmeal or eggs for myself. Sometimes all I could afford was toast with peanut butter.

Money was tight, but I made sure she always had the best of what I could give. Feedin' her felt sacred.

The way her tiny hands reached for the spoon, the way she laughed at my airplane noises—it made me forget, if only for a moment, the chaos waitin' outside our front door.

"Good job, Pooh Bear," I'd say when she finished a meal, wipin' her face with a warm cloth. "You ate it all like a big girl."

Then came the rush of packin' the diaper bag with bottles, extra clothes, wipes, and pacifier.

Then I had to pack my school bag with textbooks, notebooks, and pens—among other things. No matter how early I started, time always felt like it was runnin' laps around me. By 7:45 am we were out the door. I had her strapped to my chest, her tiny head restin' under my chin, smellin' like lotion and baby hair oil.

The air was crisp, bitin' my cheeks awake. Some mornings it rained, and I'd drape an old blanket over both of us like a makeshift shield while we waited for the bus.

Other mothers stood there too—balancin' babies, strollers, and grocery bags. We never really talked much, but there was a silent understandin' in the way we nodded at each other.

I see you. You see me. We both tired, but we moving.

The bus groaned to a stop, its brakes squealin' like a wounded animal. The driver always looked half-asleep, coffee cup balanced on the dashboard. "Morning," he'd mumble, and I'd mumble back, flashin' my pass.

The ride was never quiet. Somebody's phone blasted rap music. A baby cried. A man yelled to himself about politics nobody asked him about. But in that noise, I learned to find a strange kind of peace. I'd lean my head back, close my eyes for a few minutes, and pray the rockin' motion didn't make my baby fussy.

Sometimes, I'd catch our reflections in the scratched window—a young mama with tired eyes and a tiny, beautiful girl nestled against her. It made me both proud and sad at the same time.

Community college wasn't glamorous, but it was a lifeline. The halls smelled like cheap floor cleaner and coffee, and the classrooms buzzed with the energy of people tryna make somethin' of themselves.

Child development was my favorite class. It felt like I was learnin' the blueprint for the kind of mama I wanted to be and the kind I never had.

We talked about attachments, milestones, and behavior patterns. I scribbled notes like my life depended on it. Because in a way it did. One day, Professor Alvarez stopped me after class.

"Amber, you doing alright? I see you rushing in here, baby on your hip, barely breathing."

I laughed, tired. "I'm hangin' on."

Her eyes softened.

"You're doing more than hanging on. You're building something. Don't forget that."

Her words stayed with me all week. Nobody had never told me that before, at least not like that.

Most people just saw a young, Black, single mother and assumed failure. But she saw my potential. She saw the fight. And it lit somethin' small but steady inside me.

After school, there was no break. I headed straight to the burger joint on E. 14th.

Grease lived in that place, clingin' to my clothes like an unwanted memory. The floor was always slick, the headsets too loud, the customers too impatient.

But that paycheck, small as it was, kept the lights on and formula in my baby's bottle.

I smiled at customers even when they didn't deserve it.

I flipped burgers like my hands were a programmed machine.

I pretended the teenage boys throwin' fries at each other in the corner didn't make me want to scream.

On my 15-minute break, I'd sit on a milk crate in the back, my journal open, shoes off, toes throbbin.' I'd write about everything—the baby's first tooth, a dream I had about a beach, the way my heart still hurt when certain songs came on.

"Today I learned that survivin' ain't the same as livin.' But right now, survivin' is all I got."

When my shift ended, I'd rush to catch the last bus, prayin' Granny wasn't too worn out watchin' my baby all night.

Life was already a tightrope, but Tommy and his people kept shakin' the damn line while I was tryna balance my life.

At first, he seemed like he was goin' to step up comin' to pick up Niaomy on weekends, buyin' diapers here and there. But slowly, the cracks showed. He'd disappear for days, not answerin' his phone, only to pop back up like nothin' happened.

One weekend, he was supposed to bring Niaomy back by Sunday evenin' so I could be ready for school the next day.

No calls.

No texts.

Midnight came and went, and my heart pounded like a drum.

By Monday morning, I was furious and terrified. When he finally showed up, the sight of my baby broke me. Her clothes were wrinkled, her little shoes scuffed and dirty. Her hair hadn't been combed in days, her breath smelled sour, and she clung to me like she'd been holdin' her cries inside the whole time.

"What the hell, Tommy?!" My voice shook with rage. "You really had my baby out here like this?"

He shrugged, actin' like it was nothin.' "Man, she's fine. You bein' dramatic."

"Fine?!" I screamed. "She smell like outside and neglect! I trusted you with her!" He looked past me, dismissive.

"You don't even got no man, Amber. You should be happy somebody even want to spend time with her."

That cut deep.

My body vibrated from holdin' back tears and fists at the same time.

"You will never EVER get her like this again," I said through gritted teeth. "Not until you grow the hell up."

From that moment on, somethin' shifted in me. It wasn't about him anymore. It was about protectin' my baby at all costs even if that meant standin' alone. But Tommy's mama didn't make that easy. She started whisperin' in his ear, turnin' him against me, paintin' me like I was the villain.

"She don't really want that baby," she'd tell him.

"She out here runnin' the streets while you takin' care of her child."

All lies. Meanwhile, this woman had a house full of grown kids, all on some type of government check, food stamps, section 8, and a system built to keep her comfortable.

She didn't know my grind. She didn't know what it took for me to keep the lights on and formula stocked. While Tommy's side was burnin' one fire, Rachelle was startin' another.

Our friendship had been through so many ups and downs that it felt like a roller coaster with no brakes.

We'd laugh one day, argue the next, and act like nothin' happened the day after that.

But this time, it was different. This time, she came for my heart with a knife.

One day, I pulled up to her house. She was sittin' on the porch with her cousins, actin' standoffish like I wasn't even there.

"Yo, Rachelle," I called out, already feelin' the tension.

She glared at me. "You really gonna act like you ain't fake, Amber? Like you don't think you better than everybody?"

"What are you even talkin' about?" My stomach dropped.

"You a bum," she spat, loud enough for everyone to hear. "Always hoppin' house to house, usin' people, then playin' victim." Her words sliced through me.

The worst part? A piece of me feared she was right. Not because it was true, but because when you were already carryin' shame, it didn't take much for someone to make you bleed.

I stepped closer, my voice low but sharp. "Nah, you the fake one. You been jealous since day one. You a snake in lip gloss."

Her cousins gasped like we were in a movie scene. Rachelle stood up, nose flarin,' fists balled.

But I didn't swing.

I didn't yell.

I just looked her dead in the eyes and said, "We done." And that was that. After years of back-and-forth, the door finally slammed shut. It hurt like hell, but deep down, I knew I was finally choosin' myself.

Healin' didn't look like a yoga class or a bubble bath.

It looked like me sittin' in the therapist's office, hands clenched, voice tremblin' as I admitted out loud what I'd only ever written in my journal.

I ain't even plan to start therapy at first. I just woke up one mornin' and felt somethin' in me snap like if I didn't get help, I was gonna drown in everything I been holdin.' So, I made the call, heart beatin' fast, not even knowin' what I was gon say just knowin' I couldn't keep doin' life the same way.

"Ms. D," I whispered. "Sometimes I feel like my whole life been one long fight. And I'm tired of swingin.'"

She nodded, calm and steady.

"Then maybe it's time to stop fighting with yourself."

Those words landed in my chest heavy. I stared at the floor, feelin' my chest get tight, realizin' that was exactly why I finally walked through her door. Because that was exactly what I'd been doin,' blamin' myself for every wrong turn, every betrayal, every heartbreak.

I didn't start therapy just to talk; I came 'cause I was tired of carryin' pain that ain't never been mine to hold.

We worked on breathin.'

On boundaries.

On learning how to say no without apologizin.'

Some days I'd leave her office feelin' lighter.

Other days, I'd cry so hard in the parkin' lot that I had to sit there with the car runnin' until I could drive safely. Healin' wasn't linear. It was messy, loud, and exhaustin.' But little by little, I started believin' I deserved more than just survival.

One night, after a particularly rough session, I sat at Granny's kitchen table.

The house smelled like fried chicken and collard greens.

My baby was asleep in the next room, and the only sound was Granny hummin' softly to herself.

"Ma," I said, voice breakin.' "I'm tryin' so hard. But it feel like every time I get ahead, something knocks me back down."

Granny put down her fork and looked me dead in the eye.

"Pooh, you been fightin' battles most folks wouldn't survive. But you ain't here by accident. You here because God got somethin' big for you." I started cryin' right there at the table, shoulders shakin.'

Granny came around and hugged me, rubbin' my back like when I was a little girl.

In that moment, I felt a peace I hadn't felt in years.

Not because everything was fixed, but because I finally believed it *could* be.

The house was quiet that night.

For once, there wasn't a storm of yellin,' cryin,' or rushin.'

My baby was asleep in her crib, her chest risin' and fallin' softly, the nightlight castin' a warm glow on her tiny face.

Granny was in her room watchin' TV, the muffled sound of Judge Judy echoed through the wall.

I sat alone at the kitchen table with a cup of lukewarm tea in my hands.

The day had been long from work, school, and Tommy's drama. But there was a stillness settlin' over me that felt… different.

Like maybe, just maybe, I was done bein' at war with myself.

I opened my journal, its pages full of pain and prayers, and started to write.

"I'm tired of carryin' what ain't mine. Tired of tryin' to earn love from people who never learned to love themselves. Tired of lettin' my past write my future."

The words poured out of me like water from a busted dam. I didn't stop until my hand cramped, until my tears blurred the ink. Then I put the pen down and looked at my reflection in the dark kitchen window. For the first time in a long time, I saw *me*. Not the girl who was abused.

Not the single mom everyone whispered about. Not the hustler, the student, the fighter. Just… Amber.

And she deserved peace.

The next morning, I packed up a small bag of clothes for my baby and me.

I didn't know exactly where we were goin,' but I knew we couldn't stay in the same cycles anymore.

Granny hugged me tight, whisperin,' "Pooh, you gon' be alright. You stronger than you think."

"I know, Ma," I said, my voice shakin.' "I just… I need to do this for me. For her."

She kissed my forehead and let me go, her tears soakin' into my hair.

As I walked down those steps with my baby on my hip, I felt a mix of fear and freedom.

The world outside was cold and messy, but it was mine to face now.

Later that night, as I rocked my baby to sleep in a small, borrowed room, I whispered a vow into the dark. "No matter how hard it gets, you will never feel unloved. You will never wonder if you matter. You will never question if you're protected."

Her little hand curled around my finger like she understood, like she was sealin' the promise with me. I cried quietly, not from sadness this time, but from releasin.'

From knowin' that I didn't have to keep repeatin' the patterns that nearly destroyed me.

Healin' wasn't pretty.

It wasn't quick, clean, or easy.

But every choice I made to walk away from pain, every boundary I set, every tear I shed in therapy and in prayer, it was all proof that I was still here. Still fightin.' Still lovin.'

I realized then that survival wasn't the finish line. Livin' was. And I wanted to live.

For me.

For my baby.

For the girl inside me who never got the love she deserved. I looked out the window at the night's sky, the moon full and glowin' like a quiet reminder.

You made it this far.

Don't stop now.

I closed my eyes, took a deep breath, and let it out slowly.

The season ahead wasn't goin' to be perfect.

But it was goin' to be *mine*.

That night didn't end with celebration or fireworks.

It ended with steady footsteps forward—messy, imperfect, but strong. After I left Tommy, I was back to square one, tryna figure out how to stand on my own two feet again.

Granny was doin' what she could, watchin' Niaomy when I had job interviews or classes, but she was gettin' older and in and out of the hospital. I appreciated every bit of help she gave me, even when she was tired or sick. That woman carried me when nobody else would.

I was fillin' out applications everywhere—fast food, retail, nursing homes—anything that would keep us afloat. I'd be sittin' on the edge of the bed at night, rockin' Niaomy, whisperin,' "Mama gon' figure this out, baby." But co-parenting with Tommy? Man, that was hell.

He'd come get Niaomy and then vanish—no calls, no updates. I'd be blowin' up his phone, no answer. I'd call his family house; they'd hang up in my face or act like they ain't hear me. They had more addresses than I could keep up with, and they'd pass my daughter around from house to house like she was luggage. They wanted folks to think I didn't care, that I was some unfit mama who didn't want her child. Whole time, I was fightin' like hell just to see my baby.

Tommy's family hated me from the start, and honestly? The feelin' was mutual.

His brother, Taevon, stayed runnin' his mouth, defendin' they mama like she was the Queen of England. Me and him went back and forth plenty times because I refused to let anybody play in my face about my child.

When I finally did get Niaomy back, it broke me how she'd come home dirty, smellin' like she hadn't had a bath in days, hair dry and matted. I'd be furious, textin' Tommy paragraphs, cussin' and cryin,' but he ain't care. He'd just ignore me like my feelings didn't exist.

And my daddy, Thomas, please he wasn't watchin' no baby. One time I asked him to keep her while I went to work, and he said, "You out your rabbit-ass mind if you think I'm watching your baby. I ain't your BD." I just stared at him like, *you supposed to be her damn granddaddy.* But even that didn't move him. He was sorry at bein' a daddy and even sorrier at bein' a grandpa.

The B.S. kept pilin' up. I'd get random Facebook messages from people tellin' me they seen Tommy out with some girl, pushin' my baby in a cart at the store, or posted up outside some apartments with her barefoot, lookin' wild. Every time I heard that, it stabbed me deep. My stomach would turn 'cause I knew it was true.

That was when it hit me; I had to get on my shit for real.

I was single, stressed, tryna keep a job, and stay in school, but everything felt like it was crumblin'. Me and my daddy were always bumpin' heads, and half the time I'd be in the streets tryna make a little money, lookin' for somewhere stable to stay. It wasn't easy.

Family would pop in, offer help here and there—a couch, a meal, a couple dollars but it never lasted long. And with family, there was always drama. I was thankful, but I was tired too. I just wanted peace. I just wanted love that didn't come with conditions.

Sometimes I'd lay in bed and dream about a different life—a husband, a big house full of kids, just love all around. I didn't care about fame or bein' seen; I just wanted somebody who stayed. Somebody who made me feel safe enough to stop fightin' all the time.

But life wasn't givin' that yet. So, I kept movin,' kept prayin,' kept doin' what I had to do.

Even when I was broke. Even when I was exhausted. Even when I felt like nobody saw me but God. Life was beatin' me down from every angle.

Between Tommy's drama, school, workin' when I could, and tryna keep a roof over me and Niaomy's head, I hit a wall.

I needed a break.

Not a nap. Not a talk. A break.

I wanted to feel young again, forget about bills, heartbreak, and baby bottles.

I wanted to get drunk, dance, laugh too loud, and not think for one damn night.

So, when a girl I knew hit me up about a little function in Oakland, I thought why not. That was how it started.

I got dressed and I had me a lil' freak-a-leak short dress on with some boots that came up to my thighs. I had some bomb scalp braids that hung all the way to my thighs, pretty smile, big hoop earrings with my medusa piercin.' Some cherry lip gloss and I was out the door. I was cruisin' down international, bumpin' *I Can Tell* by 504 Boyz. I came up to a red light and my window was down. Some silver Honda pulled up next to me and it was some bad ass female I used to see around.

"Hey, Amber!" she said.

"Hey, Laysia!"

"You playing my shit!"

"Ahhhh, this my shit too."

"Where you on your way to?" she asked.

"Girl, I'm goin' to go link with a homegirl of mine from college to go dance and have drinks."

"I wanna come!"

"Ok, bet, follow me.."

We steady cruisin,' about 15 minutes away from the club we were goin' to. I was feelin' some kind of way because I already been havin' emotions about women and Laysia was super bad, but I didn't know if she swung that way. I was gon' see if she was into girls. I was not gone come on hard; I just wanted to see if she noticed what I was on when we get to the club... I was just ready to have some fun.

CHAPTER THIRTEEN

AMBER'S CROWN

Wearing my name with pride.
Finding strength in my story

The function was packed—music shakin' the walls, smoke cloudin' the air, girls in heels they couldn't walk in, and dudes flexin' like they owned the block.

I showed up with a Laysia and met up with Dashay, just tryna get out the house.

It was a vibe. We was cute as hell and it was no drama—just smiles and good vibes.

I was in my feelings and just needed to feel somethin' that wasn't pain.

Dashay was wild but funny. Me and Laysia started catchin' up and talkin.' We started drinkin' and dancin.' She began lookin' at me with these sexy eyes. Maybe it was just all in my head because I was goin' through a gay phase. They played some of the bombast music. Before I knew it, we was all tipsy and just gigglin.'

"Amber, I love you, girl," Dashay said.

"I love you too, girl."

Laysia started huggin' on me and I started gettin' butterflies. She looked me dead in my eyes.

"You so pretty, Amber."

"You pretty too, boo." Her eyes started movin' back and forth. She grabbed my hand and started walkin' toward the bathroom. She walked through the door with me behind and put her back against the wall and brought me close.

"You like girls?" she whispered.

I smiled and said I been havin' mixed feelings. She leaned up and started kissin' me. We made out for about two minutes and she began feelin' on me, all under my dress. I started gettin' all hot and horny and we went to the bathroom stall and started lickin' and fuckin' on each otha. In that moment, it felt right. It was what I needed and it was good and sweet.

We were so drunk; I didn't even know how the rest of the night went or how we got home but we did. Dashay called me the next mornin,' talkin loud and like, "Mhmm BITCH! You a freakkkk!" I busted out laughin.'

"Ain't nobody stupid. You and Miss Laysia disappeared and y'all was lookin' real gay...."

"Shut up, Dashay. We was usin' the bathroom."

"Girl, for a whole 45 minutes? Bitch please…"

I laughed it up but deep inside I had caught feelings that quick. I wasn't sure if this made me a lesbian now but I was in my feels….

After that night, Dashay started takin' me around a little bit of everywhere.

We'd hit little kickbacks, link with dudes for bottles, steal baby stuff, and snacks out the store for Niaomy. We hustled where we could.

I was still tryna stay in community college, jugglin' classes, late buses, and bad decisions. I told myself it was temporary.

Then one weekend, Dashy said,

"Sis, they having a pool party in the East and an after-party at Lux in West Oakland. You tryna go?"

I didn't even hesitate. I needed it.

We carpooled—me, Dashy, and two of her homegirls. We had our own smoke, liquor, and speakers.

By the time we pulled up to the pool party, the vibe was lit.

Music bumpin,' people dancin,' bodies glistenin' in the sun. It felt like freedom for the first time in a long time.

When the pool party ended, we slid straight to Lux Oakland, this lounge in West Oakland that stayed turnt.

The lights were low, the DJ was on point, and the men in there were fine as hell chains swingin,' smiles dangerous.

That was where I met Kameron.

He wasn't loud like the rest. He had that quiet confidence, the kind that made you look twice.

We locked eyes across the crowd, and he gave me that little half-smile that said he already knew what was up.

Before the night was over, we exchanged numbers, laughed like we'd known each other forever, and talked until the lights came on.

After that night, we couldn't stay away from each other.

Calls every day. Late-night rides.

I didn't want to get my heartbroken again by anotha nigga. I wanted to go to the otha side but deep down I knew that was not where I really wanted to be…. It was a good time and experience with Laysia, but I was a mother. Would I want that for her? Could I marry a woman? Like after that night, I hadn't seen or heard much from her. Time started movin' fast.

Within a few weeks, me and Kameron moved into a weekly motel together—young, wild, and thinkin' love could fix everything.

We told each other we loved each other like it was a promise instead of a prayer.

We was havin' sex like the world was endin,' drinkin,' vibin,' and livin' in a bubble.

But reality showed up fast.

Bills stacked. Money short. I wasn't workin' but tryna find another job.

Until then, I was talkin' to niggas for money and never had to give up no pussy, but it still felt wrong.

Embarrassin,' really.

'Cause Kameron ain't have no job either, and the little hustle he talked about was all cap.

I thought I had me a rapper-trapper type, but nah this wasn't that.

He'd sit around smokin' and playin' video games while I was stressin' over how to keep us fed.

Soon enough, we got kicked out the weekly.

Back on the hunt for another one, broke and arguin' every other day.

My attitude got bad.

His laziness started pissin' me off.

One day, we was swimmin,' tryna cool off, and I felt this sharp thumpin' pain deep in my body.

I climbed out the pool and sat there breathin' heavy, somethin' didn't feel right.

Back at the house, I kept thinkin,' *Damn… I'm late.*

I told him to grab a pregnancy test.

He came back and I took it.

Two lines.

My whole world stopped.

I walked out the bathroom in shock, holdin' the test.

He looked at me, face blank.

That was when it hit me I was pregnant again, and this time the love story already had cracks.

He was on the fence, sayin' all the right words but movin' funny.

Reality had finally caught up.

And deep down, I knew another lesson was comin.'

We quickly had a turn for the worst.

What started off sweet turned sour so damn fast, it made my head spin.

We went from long phone calls, late-night cuddles, celebratin' small wins, and really bein' there for each other to walkin' on eggshells, arguin' over nothin,' and barely wantin' to be in the same room.

What once felt like peace turned into entrapment, irritation, and resentment.

When I told Kameron's mama I was pregnant, her whole face dropped.

She said, "Y'all don't even know each other like that, and he already got a child out there he ain't even seen."

That stung, 'cause she wasn't lyin' but she wasn't bein' lovin' either.

From that day forward, everything in that house felt tense.

Some days we was cool, laughin' and jokin' like family; other days, it was straight smoke—arguments, attitude, and everybody in their feelings.

We were livin' with his mama, and it was hell.

She was one of them women who always had to be right, even when she wasn't.

She'd talk slick, then play victim when you called her out.

I was pregnant and emotional, but I wasn't no fool I peeped everything.

Me and Kameron would argue, then she'd jump in to defend him like he was ten-years-old.

It was like livin' in a house full of mirrors. Everywhere I turned, I saw my own stress starin' back at me.

After too many fights, too much tension, I packed my stuff and left.

I ended up movin' in with a woman I called Auntie Minnie.

She wasn't blood, but she was realer than half my family.

I met her on the bus years ago and we clicked instantly.

She had this loud laugh and a good spirit that could light up a cloudy day.

Auntie Minnie didn't have much, but what she had, she shared. She'd say, "Baby, you can stay here as long as you need. I know what it's like to start over."

And she meant that.

I loved that woman to death. She gave me peace when everything else was chaotic.

Now my daddy, that was a different story.

He'd be there for everybody else but me.

He'd go help cousins move, drop off money to other folks, and play hero for the world but when it came to me, suddenly I was "too much."

He'd tell people I was disrespectful, hard-headed, ungrateful, paintin' this fake picture like I was the problem.

Never once did he mention the things he said to me or how cold he could be.

Typical covert narcissistic parent the kind that hurts you, then made you apologize for bleedin.'

He'd say things like, "You need to fix your attitude." When all I wanted was for him to act like a father. It was like I could never win. The same man that told me to be strong was the one who broke me the most.

Sometimes, I'd sit in Auntie Minnie's livin' room, hand on my stomach, thinkin' about how I was really doin' this on my own again.

Pregnant, heart bruised, tryna build a future off broken pieces.

But I told myself, "You been through worse. You'll make it through this, too."

And I meant it.

Because no matter who stayed or who switched up, I was still standin.'

After I moved in with Auntie Minnie, things were still rocky.

People kept sayin,' *"You can come stay with me if you need to,"* but when the time came, they'd switch up. Phone on DND. Excuses ready.

It was always somethin,' "Oh, I gotta ask my dude," "My kids too much," "Maybe next week."

They'd talk that love talk, but when I really needed somewhere to go, it was crickets.

I was meetin' different people through my struggle, callin' them family 'cause sometimes strangers held you down harder than blood ever would.

I'd crash on couches, floors—wherever I could fit.

Some days I woke up refreshed, ready to start over.

Other days I was numb, tired of beggin' life to give me a break.

It was a lot of drama in these streets.

People smiled in your face, then threw salt the second you walked away.

Some nights, I'd rather sleep in the car just to get away from the noise, the arguments, the fake energy.

Even though me and Kameron weren't livin' together full-time, he'd still come with me to the ultrasound appointments.

I had to get another cerclage, and it hurt just like the first one.

Every time, I'd lay there prayin,' hopin' this baby made it through.

And of course, another C-section was waitin' on me at the end.

It was the most uncomfortable pregnancy I ever had emotionally and physically.

People hated me and Kameron together.

His friends said I was a distraction, my so-called friends said I was stupid.

It was negativity comin' from every direction.

Even people who claimed they were happy for me had shade in their smiles.

I learned quickly fake love was louder than real support.

We struggled hard that whole pregnancy.

Most of the time, we were in separate houses, barely talkin' unless it was somethin' important.

We'd meet up for appointments, baby showers, or family stuff, but deep down we both knew we wasn't really together anymore.

We had love, but it was buried under stress and resentment.

We were just tryna survive; two broken people holdin' onto what was left of a dream that never had a solid start.

There were nights I'd sit in the dark rubbin' my belly, thinkin' about how different this pregnancy felt.

No excitement. No fairy tale. Just survival mode.

I'd text him sometimes, tryna keep the peace, but we'd end up arguin' about nothin.'

I was emotional, tired, and lonely.

He was distant, cold, like he already checked out.

We never really went on dates.

We'd talk about doin' something nice, but it never happened.

We tried to celebrate each other's birthdays, but it always turned into an argument.

I'd cry, he'd get quiet.

I needed affection, he needed space.

We were livin' in two different worlds, callin' it love.

I wanted to believe we could fix it, that maybe once the baby came things would change but deep down I knew better.

Sometimes you could love somebody and still knew they ain't the one you supposed to build with.

That was a pain only grown women understood.

Still, I kept goin.'

Even when I was broke, even when I was drained, even when it felt like everyone was against me, I kept choosin' life.

For me.

For my kids.

For the woman I was still becomin.'

By the time I met Kameron, Granny was already gone.

That grief was a quiet shadow I carried everywhere.

She was my backbone; the one who saw through my attitude and still loved me out loud.

Losin' her cracked somethin' in me I didn't know how to fix.

So when life threw another pregnancy my way, I had to face it raw—no guidance, no safety net, just me tryna make sense of the silence she left behind.

The first few days after Celeste came into the world felt unreal.

The hospital smelled like bleach and sadness; the beepin' machines became my new soundtrack.

Every time the nurse checked my pressure or my incision, I winced and smiled through it, actin' tougher than I felt.

But when they placed her in my arms—6 pounds, 15 ounces of soft brown skin and steady breath—somethin' inside me unclenched.

Her cry wasn't loud, but it was sure like she already knew she was meant to be here.

For a few days, Kameron showed up like the man I prayed for.

He held her, took pictures, told the nurses how proud he was.

We laughed in the hospital room like maybe we could start over.

But once we got home, the peace wore off fast.

My body was weak, but my mind was runnin' miles.

Tryna heal from bein' cut open in the same place twice, tryna nurse a newborn, tryna keep Niaomy from feelin' forgotten. It was too much for one person, but I didn't have a choice.

The nights were long.

The house stayed quiet except for the baby's soft cries and the hum of the TV.

I'd sit in the dark, feedin' Celeste with one hand and wipin' my face with the other.

There was no one to call.

No Granny's voice sayin,' *"Baby, breathe. You gon' be fine."*

Just me and my thoughts, heavy as the air around me.

Kameron started fadin' before my body even finished healin.'

He'd leave late, come back later, smellin' like smoke and outside.

When I'd ask where he been, he'd say, *"Chillin,'"* like that explained the ache sittin' in my chest.

He'd laugh with his friends over the phone while I rocked a cryin' baby, stitches pullin' every time I stood up.

We were sharin' space, not a life.

I wanted partnership; he wanted peace and quiet.

I wanted help; he wanted freedom.

And that gap between us just kept stretchin.'

Some mornings I'd look in the mirror and not recognize myself.

Eyes swollen, lips dry, soul somewhere far behind my reflection.

That scar on my stomach felt like a branded proof of what I'd endured and everything I couldn't erase.

I'd trace it with my fingers and whisper, "You still here, girl. You still here."

But the truth was, I didn't feel alive.

I was functionin.'

Breathin.'

Existin.'

People thought I was strong, but strength didn't always mean peace.

It just meant you learned how to survive without applause.

One night, Celeste started cryin,' and I picked her up slowly, my body still sore but my spirit wide awake.

The TV light flickered over Kameron knocked out on the couch, controller hangin' from his hand like another promise he dropped.

I looked at him not out of anger, but acceptance.

He wasn't evil, just lost.

And I was tired of tryna build love on top of brokenness.

I held Celeste close and whispered into her hair, "Mama gon' get it right one day. You deserve peace. We all do."

Then I laid her down beside me, pulled the blanket over us, and stared at the ceilin' till the tears stopped burnin.'

The pain was still there, but it didn't own me anymore.

I'd been cut, opened, stitched, and scarred and somehow, I was still standin.'

That was my reminder.

That was my proof.

And that night, for the first time in a long time, I didn't feel afraid.

I just felt ready.

Let me tell you somethin.'

Life gone life.

It's gone hit you when you least expect it, knock you flat on your back, and wait to see if you get up.

And when you do?

You come back wiser, louder, stronger, and with a testimony that ain't just yours but for everybody else watchin.'

This chapter right here ain't just for me.

It's for every young, Black girl or woman who's ever been told she was too much.

Too loud. Too broken. Too "fast." Too far gone.

It's for every Black mama out there holdin' it down with no help.

Every sister, daughter, cousin, friend, or anybody tryna survive a storm and still believe the sun will shine again.

I'm here to tell you, you can go through it, pray through it, and grow through it.

You don't gotta be perfect.

You just gotta keep goin.'

So, he'd stay in the house all day, smokin,' playin' video games, sleepin,' then takin' the car for hours.

I'd be at home barefoot, swollen, stomach tight, standin' over a hot ass stove just to make sure we ate.

Then cleanin' up, doin' laundry, changin' diapers all while he out with his boys or talkin' bout,

"I just needed to get some air."

Nah. You needed to be a man.

It got to the point where my doctor told me I had to stop workin.'

Immediately.

I'd be layin' there in pain—tired, emotionally drained—and he talkin' bout, "Come here."

Boy, if you don't get yo…

We started arguin' every day.

Screamin,' cussin.' My mouth was wild, and my temper?

Shorter than a midget on his knees.

But Kameron wasn't the type to take shit either.

He'd snap right back. Sometimes, he'd leave for hours after an argument, take the car, and wouldn't check in.

Our love started rottin' from the inside.

And when the money ran out, so did the little bit of peace we had left.

We lost everything.

And just like that, we were homeless.

No money.

No place to go.

Nowhere stable for me to lay down and carry this baby.

Let me pause right here and say this.

To the women out there who feel like they losin,' you're not.

You're learnin.'

You're buildin' grit.

You're findin' out who you are when everything around you crumbles.

You don't gotta have it all figured out.

You don't gotta be soft all the time.

You don't gotta be perfect to be powerful.

But you do gotta keep goin.'

Because one day, all of them sleepless nights, all of them tears, all of those moments when you prayed with a dry mouth and a broken spirit, will start makin' sense.

Let me know when you're ready to keep buildin' from here; we can go into how y'all survived being homeless, who helped and who didn't, how your faith kept you grounded, and what you started to realize about yourself as a woman, a mama, and a future boss.

You're not just tellin' a story; you're writin' a manual for survival and transformation. And every page hits.

Let me tell you somethin,' life don't come with no manual, especially when you a Black girl just tryna make it out the mud.

Life gon' test you, try you, flip you upside down, and dare you to fight back.

And me?

I fought back every damn time.

This ain't just my story; it's a message.

For every woman, every mama, every girl who feel like she done hit rock bottom and got folks standin' around whisperin,' "she ain't gone make it."

Bitch, watch me.

You gon' go through it.

But if you have any God in you, any fire in your soul, any ounce of fight left?

You gon' pray through it.

And eventually, you gon' grow through it.

Because even when you don't feel like it, you still have purpose.

Now by this time, me and Kameron was down bad.

Real bad.

I'd be out workin' two jobs, feet swollen, back screamin,' tryin' to do the right thing...

and I'd come home to this dude in his drawers, controller in one hand, blunt in the other, talkin' 'bout, "What we eatin' tonight?"

Nigga, shut yo ass up.

I was the one bustin' my ass and he was laid up like I adopted him.

I'd be the one cleanin,' cookin,' and takin' care of my daughter, damn near beggin' him to wash a plate or check the mail.

But he'd roll up, play 2K, and act like it was enough just to breathe in my presence.

Then came the moment that broke me. Sittin' in a dusty ass room, I was worried 'bout how we gon' eat, where the rent comin' from, and how I was goin' keep my baby safe...

And Kameron?

Still tryna fuck.

"Aight, damn. You actin' like I can't touch you."

"Boy, shut yo ass up before I knock you through this wall."

One day, we damn near tore the room apart.

And when the money ran out, when the savings dried up like old paint...

We lost it all.

Had to pack our shit up and go.

No backup plan.

No stable family to run to.

Just us. And homelessness.

Baby in my belly.

To every Black woman readin' this listen to me.

I don't care how low you fall, how lonely it get, how heavy that baby feel in your belly or on your hip, you can get through it.

Don't let nobody tell you what you can't survive.

They said I was too loud, too hood, too reckless, too broken.

But guess what?

I'm still here.

And I ain't never folded.

God don't ask you to be perfect.

He just ask you to show up.

Even if you cryin.' Even if you cussin.' Even if your voice shakes.

Just. Show. Up.

After we lost everything, Kameron went to his mama's house, and I packed up my daughter, my pregnant belly, and went over to my Auntie Franny's. She welcomed me with open arms—no judgment, no backhanded comments, just love. A bed. A door I could close. Peace.

I couldn't go to Kameron's mama's house, and truth be told, I ain't want to.

She ain't like me, so I ain't want to hear a damn thing about her askin' for baby updates.

If you didn't like me, you didn't like my babies. Period.

So, I kept my distance.

I let Kameron deal with her. I needed peace more than fake concern.

At Auntie Franny's, I finally had a room to lay down in. A little corner of the world to breathe in.

No drama, no yellin,' no tension.

Just me, my baby, and my belly.

Kameron and I only linked when it came to doctor's appointments.

We had lost our car, so it was hard, but we made it work when we had to.

Other than that? He was at his mama's. I was at my auntie's. We were driftin.'

During that time, I started doin' what I knew best, poured into myself.

I read books. I prayed.

Held my daughter's hand every day, walked her to school. Talked to her about life in the little ways I could.

Meanwhile, Tommy had a new girlfriend.

He and her had moved in together.

At first, I didn't want my baby goin' over there.

But my daughter was innocent. She didn't understand grown folks' problems.

So eventually, I gave in.

I let him take her.

Because once again, I didn't have family support, and as much as I hated it, he was still her father.

I had long been done with him emotionally.

There was no love left.

He played in my face, acted like he wanted peace, and co-parenting, but the whole time I was strugglin' and fightin' through my pregnancy, tryna stay afloat on government assistance. Come to find out, this man was buildin' a legal case behind my back.

Tryna take my baby away.

He knew how my family was. He knew my situation.

Still, instead of helpin,' he was plottin.'

I had cash aid. EBT. Food stamps.

That was how I survived.

Kameron had no job, no money, no stability.

Hell, he had warrants. Legal shit always swirlin' around him like a bad omen. Then one morning, around 10 AM, Tommy pulled up to pick up Niaomy.

I packed her backpack, gave her a kiss, handed her over and just like that...

I wouldn't see my daughter for the next four months.

I called.

No answer.

Called again. Straight to voicemail.

Then one day, I called and a woman answered.

"Hello?"

"Hello... is Tommy there?"

"No... he's not."

"Okay... um, who is this?"

"I'm Bri."

I sat there, heat risin' in my chest.

"Bri? Okay well... since you're there, and my daughter's clearly with y'all, you already in this, so let's talk." She paused. I could hear the nervousness in her voice.

"I don't wanna be in y'all mess..."

"Too late, baby girl. My daughter been at y'all house. So what's up?" She started openin' up. Hesitant, but honest.

"Tommy's barely around. I have her most of the time. His mama? She always bossin' me around, reminding me I'm not Niaomy's mama. But like... where is Tommy?"

I gave her the whole play.

"That woman is a snake. She's sneaky, conniving, a whole addict. She lies just to lie. Lives through her kids cause she ain't never had her own life. She hates me, so she'll say anything to make me look bad."

Bri went quiet for a second.

"OMG... I knew something was off. I noticed it after like six months of being with Tommy. She's so possessive. She told me you were crazy, said you was gon' try to fight me, told me I was obsessed with Tommy."

"Of course she did. That's her M.O. Keep people blind so she can pull the strings."

"Ughhh, I hate that bitch."

Then she told me somethin' that had me ready to burn it all down.

"She called the welfare office on you."

"What?!"

"Yeah. She said you don't have your daughter, that you're lazy, and they were gonna cut your assistance off."

That was my last straw. I had to call and clear everything up, fight for my daughter, and my damn survival.

Bri kept goin.'

"Tommy doesn't bathe her. Doesn't brush her hair. Feed her sweets all day. He's not a good father."

"Loving your daughter and being a parent ain't the same thing. He wants credit for just showing up."

She sighed.

"And God, she looks just like him…"

I felt that in my soul.

This was the life I was livin.'

Pregnant. Strugglin.' Lied on. Battlin' for the child I carried and birthed.

And still wakin' up every mornin', thankin' God for breath in my lungs and strength in my bones. Because no matter how many times they tried to break me, I didn't fold.

After I hung up with Bri, I sat there shakin.' I had enough. I called the police and asked for a welfare check on my daughter. I explained everything—how I hadn't seen her in four months, how her father was keepin' her from me, how she was livin' in a house full of people who didn't give a damn about her well-bein.'

They came out, did the check, and then told me, "Ma'am, you're going to have to handle this through family court."

My heart dropped.

Court? Lawyers? More time? More money I didn't have.

I wanted to scream but before I could even process that...

My phone rang.

This time it was the hospital.

"Ms. Crown, your grandmother has been admitted to Kaiser Medical Center. You need to come quickly."

My world stopped.

"What?! What's wrong?!"

"She's very ill. Please get here as soon as you can."

I turned to Auntie Franny, tears already burnin' behind my eyes.

"Auntie... Granny's back in the hospital. We gotta go. NOW!"

We flew down the freeway, hearts poundin,' stomachs in knots.

When we walked into that hospital room, my soul cracked wide open.

There she was...

My granny. My rock. My everything.

Laid out in that bed.

Pale. Weak. Confused.

She didn't even know who was comin' or goin.'

They said her cancer had reached stage 4...

And now, on top of that, she was battlin' dementia.

I couldn't breathe.

I couldn't think.

I dropped to my knees next to her bed. "Ma... please... GET BETTER! GOD, HEAL MY MAMA! PLEASE!"

She was in and out of it—eyes driftin,' voice low.

She'd say my name one minute, then forget who I was the next.

And then the doctor came in with that damn clipboard and that hollow face that already told me the truth before he even opened his mouth.

"We're sorry, but the cancer has spread. At this point, it's terminal. She has... maybe three months. Could be less."

I lost it.

Screamed.

Cried.

Tripped out.

Broke down.

I couldn't imagine a world without my granny.

The only one who'd been there since day one.

The only one who watched Niaomy without complaint.

The only one who slid me a few dollars when I was dead broke.

The only one who truly loved me without condition.

She was the only one who loved my baby like her own.

When nobody else gave a fuck, Granny did.

When I had no food, Granny cooked.

When I had no ride, Granny figured it out.

And now…

She was dyin.'

By this time, Niaomy was almost two.

The years had flown by.

So much drama.

So many betrayals.

So many family feuds and fake "co-parenting" setups that only served to hurt me and confuse my daughter.

Enough was enough.

I was tired of hidin,' manipulatin,' the lies, the control.

Tommy wasn't no damn father.

He was just another man usin' his child as a pawn to hurt the woman he couldn't control no more.

And me?

I was a damn good mother.

No help.

No breaks.

No village.

Just me, my baby, and God.

I did everything I could for my daughter.

I missed out on friendships, holidays, fun, peace, freedom but I never let her go without.

I did somethin' some women weren't able to do and no matter who her father was or what we had been through, I was a proud mother. Life was hard, but Niaomy was joy. She was light. She made me want to be better, be stronger, and show up different. Because my mama wasn't there for me, and I swore to God I was gonna be there for my baby.

Children made you grow up real fast.

They changed your body, your thinkin,' the way you moved through this world.

That C-section pain wasn't no joke. Neither was healin' from a cerclage. Add to that the sleepless nights, diapers, cluster feedings, tryna shower while the baby cried in the background and still not havin' a partner to support you? It was all overwhelmin.'

Everything was expensive. I had to collect TANF and food stamps for a while because I couldn't work. I was strugglin.' But I was still showin' up. Still learnin.' Still standin' on my own.

And through all that pain, I found purpose.

I found love I didn't even know was possible.

I wasn't goin' let Tommy and his family destroy me and trick me out of raisin' my daughter

And now?

Now I was twenty-three-years-old, pregnant, broke, and about to lose the only woman in the world who ever showed me what love really looked like.

I sat in that hospital room, holdin' her hand, and I said it out loud.

"Granny… I can't make it without you. You're all I got. You and Niaomy… y'all the only ones that ever truly loved me. What am I supposed to do now?"

She didn't respond.

But she squeezed my hand—weak, soft, and full of all the love I'd been chasin' from everybody else.

I found myself wakin' up in the middle of the night still in that stiff-ass hospital chair next to Granny's bed. The room was quiet, just the steady beeps of machines and the low hum of air conditionin.' But my chest was loud.

My heart was poundin.'

My spirit was achin.'

I looked over at her—still.

Too still.

Like the breath in her body was borrowed and God could come collect at any moment.

I got up, tiptoed into the hallway, slid down the wall, and sat on that cold ass floor with my head in my hands.

And then… I prayed.

"God… I know everything got a season.

And I know life and death sit in your hands. But please… just prepare me.

I don't know how to say goodbye. I don't know how to lose the one person who never gave up on me. Please, give me peace if you gotta take her. Please, give me strength if I gotta walk without her. Don't let this pain turn me into someone I don't recognize."

I sat there in silence, hopin' for something, anything, that would calm the storm in my chest.

Then I pulled my phone out and searched for scriptures to prepare for death.

And this one popped up like God placed it there just for me:

"For I am now ready to be offered, and the time of my departure is at hand. I have fought a good fight, I have finished my course, I have kept the faith," 2 Timothy 4:6-7 (KJV).

I read it over and over.

I have fought a good fight. I have finished my course. I have kept the faith.

And that was Granny.

She had been fightin' her whole life.

Raisin' kids that wasn't hers. Feedin' folks that wouldn't feed her back.

Holdin' down the whole family with prayers, Cool 100s, and casseroles. She kept the faith.

Even when her body was givin' out.

Even when her memory started slippin.'

Even when the world treated her like she was disposable.

I went back into the room, wiped my face, and leaned down by her bed.

"Ma… I'm not ready. But I trust you fought your fight. Just stay a lil longer if you can… but if you gotta go. I'll keep the faith for the both of us."

The next morning, the hospital told us they were gettin' ready to transfer my granny to hospice.

My chest got tight. Hospice meant there was no comin' back.

The family started comin' in from all over New York, parts of Cali. There were people I hadn't seen in years.

My dad and his girlfriend popped in and out, too. Everybody wanted to say their goodbyes before it was too late.

Meanwhile, I was still tryna hold down life on my end. I went to family court, filed paperwork on Tommy, tryna get my baby back doin' everything I could not to fall apart completely.

After court, I met up with Kameron. He told me he had finally found a part-time job doin' home healthcare, helpin' his mama. But even that felt half-hearted because she was splittin' the check with him and writin' it off like he was doin' the most. Anything to keep him dependent on her.

He gave me what little he could, but it wasn't enough. It was bare minimum.

And the truth was… he didn't know my granny.

He came into my life at the end, durin' the storm, and everything between us had been struggle after struggle.

Granny knew I was pregnant. But she wasn't fully here anymore.

Some days, she'd smile at my belly. Other days, she looked right through me.

As the visits continued and her memory slipped more and more, I started buildin' a plan in my head. I had to get the fuck up outta Oakland.

It was too much.

Fake ass friends, nothing-ass niggas, family who only show up when there was a photo opp.

No matter how many jobs I worked…

How many classes I took…

How many sacrifices I made…

Oakland was heavy.

From gangbanging, to hittin' licks, to sleepin' in cars, fightin' demons in silence, bein' a young mama with no help, losin' more than I ever gained…

But still, I stood tall.

I had my strength.

I had my voice.

And soon… I'd have my second baby girl.

Two months passed.

I was out at the store, pickin' up a few things when my phone rang.

I answered, not thinkin' anything of it.

But on the other end, the nurse said words I'd never forget. "Ms. Crown… your grandmother has passed. You need to come now."

My heart hit the floor.

I screamed right there in the aisle.

Dropped everything.

Ran out of the store like I couldn't breathe. "NOOOOO! MA!!! PLEASE!!"

My Auntie Franny drove like her soul was on fire.

We flew down the freeway to the hospice center, pulled into the lot, ran through the automatic doors, and jumped on the elevator.

When the doors opened, there stood my daddy.

Hat low. Black shades. Head down. Silent.

He looked at me and just said, "Come on, baby. She's in her room."

My knees damn near gave out.

I walked in…

And there she was.

My granny. My world.

Lyin' still. Peaceful.

Gone.

I collapsed.

"Mama, noooo. Mama please. Just wait. WAIT FOR ME! Please don't leave yet!"

I sobbed like my body couldn't hold it all.

The room filled with cries—snot, tears, broken hearts everywhere.

They handed me all her personal belongings in a bag. Her rings. Her Bible. Her perfume. The little things that smelled like home.

I started havin' flashbacks.

Her brushin' my hair.

Cookin' pork chops and rice.

Sneakin' me snacks.

Tellin' me I was smart when nobody else saw it.

Holdin' me when the world treated me like nothin.'

And now…

I wasn't gon' see her again.

Not for a very, very long time.

I bent down one last time.

Gave her a kiss on her soft, wrinkled cheek.

"Save me a spot in heaven, Granny. You were everything to me."

Then I whispered to myself the verse that played over and over in my mind, "To be absent from the body is to be present with the Lord," 2 Corinthians 5:8 (KJV).

I didn't know how I was gonna keep going…

But I knew I had to.

For her.

For me.

For my girls.

Granny's crown didn't fall; it was passed down.

And now?

It was my time to wear it.

CHAPTER FOURTEEN

THIS IS WHO I AM

Owning every scar. Every setback. Every survival

The morning of my granny's funeral, the sky was gray and heavy like it already knew the world was losin' one of its brightest stars.

I woke up before the sun, lyin' still in bed with tears already soakin' my pillow. It was like my body knew this was the last day I'd ever see her face.

The house felt hollow without her hummin' gospel songs or fussin' at me to get up and get ready. Even the walls seemed to ache.

I dressed slowly, carefully, like if I moved too fast the whole day would crumble.

I slipped into a black fitted dress she would've loved, pulled my hair back into a sleek bun, and stared at my reflection in the mirror.

I didn't recognize myself.

My eyes were puffy, my shoulders tense, my mouth set in a straight line like I was tryna hold back everything I felt inside.

My daughter toddled over to me, clutchin' her little stuffed bear.

She was too young to understand what was happenin,' but her presence reminded me that life was still movin,' still demandin' I keep goin,' even when I didn't want to.

"Come on, baby girl," I whispered, pickin' her up. "We gotta say goodbye to Granny."

The church was packed wall-to-wall.

Family, friends, neighbors, and everyone who had ever been touched by my granny's kindness showed up. The air smelled like flowers, perfume, and grief. Soft music played in the background from the organ as ushers guided people to their seats.

I walked in and immediately felt a lump form in my throat.

There she was, lyin' in her casket, dressed in her Sunday's best.

Her hands folded neatly, her face peaceful, almost like she was just restin.'

But I knew better.

I knew she was gone.

My knees buckled, and I had to grab the edge of the pew to keep from fallin.'

My cousin wrapped an arm around me, whisperin,' "You got this, Amber. She'd want you to be strong."

Strong.

That word again.

Everybody always tellin' me to be strong like it was some magic switch I could just turn on.

When it was time to speak, I walked up to the podium; my hands shook so bad, I could barely hold the paper.

I looked out at the sea of faces, most of them red-eyed and tear-streaked, and then back at my granny.

"She wasn't just my grandmother," I began, my voice trembling. "She was my safe place. My protector. The one person who loved me even when I didn't know how to love myself."

I paused, swallowin' the lump in my throat.

"She taught me how to survive, but she also taught me how to fight for more than just survival. She showed me what love looked like, even when the world felt cold."

By the time I finished, there wasn't a dry eye in the room.

Even some of the men who swore they "didn't cry" were wipin' their faces.

As the choir sang *Amazing Grace*, we filed past her casket one last time.

I kissed her forehead, whisperin,' "I love you, Ma. Thank you for everything."

Walkin' out of that church felt like walkin' out of a chapter of my life I wasn't ready to close.

Funerals had a way of bringing out the truth in people.

Some showed up just to be seen, whisperin' behind fans, actin' like they cared when they hadn't called in years.

Old wounds bubbled to the surface.

Cousins who hadn't spoken in forever exchanged cold looks, and certain family members couldn't resist slidin' in slick comments about who was and wasn't really there for Granny.

I stayed quiet, holdin' my baby close because that day wasn't about them.

But inside, I was boilin.'

Granny had been the glue holdin' us all together, and now that she was gone, I could already feel the cracks widenin.'

It was like the whole family was a house built on shaky foundation, and we were finally seein' where it was ready to crumble.

The days that followed were a blur.

I moved through them like a ghost, doin' the bare minimum to keep my daughter fed and the lights on.

Every corner of the house reminded me of her.

The rockin' chair by the window.

The smell of her perfume lingerin' in the hallway.

The old Bible she kept on the kitchen table, pages worn and marked with handwritten notes.

I'd catch myself pickin' up the phone to call her, only to remember she wasn't there.

It hurt in ways I didn't even have words for.

People checked in for a week or two, bringin' food, callin' to see if I was okay.

But then, like always, they faded back into their own lives, leavin' me to navigate the grief alone.

One night, I sat in the dark livin' room, rockin' my daughter to sleep, and whispered, "It's just us now, baby. We gotta be strong. For Granny."

But my words felt hollow.

Even my daughter, though she didn't fully understand, seemed to notice the emptiness.

She'd wander around the house callin' for "G.G," her little voice echoin' through the quiet rooms, and it shattered me every time.

Just when I thought I couldn't take any more pain, life threw another curveball.

My daughter had been strugglin' with certain milestones—walkin,' talkin,' respondin' to her name.

At first, I brushed it off.

"Kids grow at their own pace," I told myself.

But deep down, I knew somethin' wasn't right.

Her daycare teacher pulled me aside one afternoon, concern etched on her face.

"Amber, I think you should get her evaluated. She's showing signs of developmental delays."

My stomach dropped.

"What do you mean delays?"

"It might be nothing," she said gently. "But it's better to check now."

I nodded, but inside, panic was risin' like floodwater.

The doctor's appointment felt like a blur.

Bright lights, cold exam tables, the smell of disinfectant.

I held my daughter close while the doctor asked questions, tested her reflexes, and observed her behavior.

When he finally sat down with his clipboard, his expression told me everything before he even spoke. "Your daughter has an intellectual disability," he said carefully.

The room spun.

My ears rang.

It felt like someone had punched me in the chest.

Intellectual disability.

Words that felt like a life sentence.

I held my baby tighter, tears streamin' down my face.

"No," I whispered. "No, there's gotta be a mistake."

The doctor shook his head gently. "It's not a mistake. But with therapy and early intervention, she can thrive. It won't be easy, but she has you. That's the most important thing."

I nodded numbly, but inside I was crumblin.'

The weeks that followed were some of the hardest of my life.

Appointments, therapy sessions, mountains of paperwork.

Learnin' new ways to communicate with my baby, new strategies to help her navigate the world.

Some days, she'd look at me with those big eyes, and I'd feel both hope and heartbreak.

Hope because she was still my baby, perfect in her own way.

Heartbreak because I knew the world wouldn't see her like I did.

I became her biggest advocate, her loudest voice.

If a teacher underestimated her, I spoke up.

If a doctor brushed her off, I demanded answers.

But behind closed doors, I fell apart.

The grief of losin' my granny mixed with the fear of my daughter's future was overwhelmin.'

Late at night, I'd sit on the bathroom floor, cryin' silently so she wouldn't hear me.

I'd pray, beg, and plead for strength.

"God, please," I whispered. "Give me what I need to be her mama. She deserves better than this world."

Over time, I started to find small victories.

The first time my daughter used sign language to ask for juice, I cried tears of joy.

The first time she laughed at a silly face I made, my heart soared.

These moments reminded me that progress didn't have to look like everyone else's timeline.

It was ours.

Slow, steady, beautiful.

My therapist helped me untangle the guilt I carried the guilt of not noticin' sooner, the guilt of sometimes feelin' overwhelmed, and the guilt of wantin' a break.

"You can't pour from an empty cup," she reminded me. "You're doing the best you can."

For the first time in a long time, I believed her.

One evening, as the sun set outside our window, I sat with my daughter in my lap.

We watched the sky turn from pink to orange to deep purple.

I thought about Granny, about everything she taught me.

About how she always said, *"Life ain't never gon' be easy, Pooh. But you gotta keep showing up."*

And that was exactly what I was doin,' showin' up.

For my baby.

For myself.

For the future we both deserved.

I kissed my daughter's forehead and whispered, "We gon' be alright. Granny's watchin' over us."

In that moment, I felt a sense of peace settle over me.

Not because everything was fixed, but because I knew we had the strength to face whatever came next.

CHAPTER FIFTEEN

BLOODLINES & BATTLE WOUNDS

Family ties, broken bonds, and choosing peace over pain

As if jugglin' Niaomy's diagnosis and Tommy was still a storm cloud hoverin' over my life.

He would pop in and out, inconsistent as ever.

One week, he'd act like super dad showin' up on time, bringin' snacks and toys, talkin' about all the things he wanted to do for our daughter.

The next week, he'd vanish without a trace, leavin' me to explain to Niaomy why her daddy didn't come.

Each time, she'd wait by the window, her little face pressed against the glass, and my heart would break a little more.

I tried to keep things peaceful for her sake.

I bit my tongue when he was late.

I stayed calm when he made excuses.

But inside, every broken promise was cuttin' me deeper, leavin' invisible scars that no one could see.

I kept askin' myself why I allowed it.

Why I kept hopin' he would change when deep down I knew exactly who he was.

It wasn't about me anymore; it was about Niaomy.

I didn't want her growin' up without her father the way I did.

I didn't want her to carry that hole in her heart.

So, I tolerated his inconsistency, even though it cost me pieces of myself every single time.

Then came the day everything changed.

It was a rainy Saturday morning, the kind where the sky seemed to pour down everything I was feelin' inside.

I stood by the window, arms crossed, watchin' for his car.

Niaomy was by the door, her little backpack on, bouncin' with excitement.

She hadn't seen her dad in two weeks, and she kept chantin,' "Daddy coming, Daddy coming!"

Her voice was full of hope, the kind only a child could have the kind that made you want to believe, too.

I'd been watchin' the clock, waitin' for the sound of his car in the driveway. My stomach turned as each minute passed, prayin' Niaomy would come back to me the way she left.

We been waitin' on him all day literally.

Niaomy kept runnin' to the window every five minutes, feet kickin,' knees bouncin,' whole body full of excitement he didn't even earn. She had her lil backpack sittin' by the door, coat on the couch, shoes halfway on... ready.

"Mommy, Daddy comin' now?"

Her voice was so hopeful; it stabbed me a lil every time.

I kept tellin' her yes, even though in my chest I already knew we was settin' ourselves up.

Hours rolled by.

Sun went down.

Neighbors pulled in.

Cars passed.

Still no sign of him.

Then finally headlights swept across the blinds.

My stomach hit the floor.

"He here, baby," I whispered.

She shot out the door like a track star, smile big as Texas, not even waitin' on me.

Tommy barely nodded. Didn't ask about her coat, didn't ask about her snacks, nothin.'

Just opened the back door like he was pickin' up a package.

Then they pulled off.

And I stood there, prayin' he'd at least treat her like somebody's child.

One day turned to two…

Two turned to four…

Then a whole damn week gone by.

No pictures.

No real updates.

Just half-ass replies, "She good." "We chillin." "She fine."

My spirit kept feelin' heavier by the day.

A mama always knew.

Then headlights again.

My heart damn near stopped.

Before I could turn the knob, Niaomy was already runnin' outside, happy just to come home.

But when she climbed out that backseat…

I swear my soul cracked.

Her hair was matted like she been layin' on the same pillow for a week straight.

Clothes dirty like she wore them to sleep, woke up in 'em, and wore 'em right back out.

Her socks stiff.

Shoes mismatch not by accident because nobody gave a damn enough to help her.

And then the smell hit me.

Not no playground smell.

Not outside smell.

This was old, heavy, sour, sittin'-on-skin-for-days type smell.

The kind that tell a story before anybody opened their mouth.

I bent down slow.

"Baby… when the last time you had a bath?"

She shrugged. Eyes dropped. Shoulders sunk.

Like she was ashamed.

Like it was her fault.

Somethin' snapped in me so hard; it felt like a bone breakin.'

I stood up, heart beatin' crazy, and faced Tommy.

"You really had my daughter lookin' like this?" My voice wasn't loud it was sharp. The kind that cut.

"Her hair. Her clothes. Her smell. She look like she been left on her own. What's wrong witchu?"

He leaned on the car like I was doin' too much.

"Man, she fine. She with me."

"Fine?!" I stepped closer. "You kept her a whole week and couldn't brush her hair? Couldn't bathe her? Couldn't make sure she straight? You think bein' a daddy is just pickin' her up and showin' her off? Nah. That ain't it."

"Here you go. You just bitter." He rolled his eyes.

That was his go-to.

Blame me.

Flip it.

Acted like he the victim.

But I wasn't swallowin' none of that no more.

"Nah, I ain't bitter," I said, voice steady but my hands shakin.' "I'm tired. I'm the one doin' everything. I'm the one talkin' to teachers. I'm the one in therapy offices. I'm the one fillin' out paperwork. I'm the one raisin' her."

I pointed at the car.

"You out here playin' pretend. I'm the one showin' up for real."

He opened his mouth to clap back…

But nothin' came out.

Just silence.

And in that silence?

I felt somethin' loosen in my chest; somethin' I been holdin' for years.

I wasn't scared of him no more.

I wasn't protectin' his feelings no more.

I wasn't hidin' the truth no more.

That was the moment I knew.

I was done lettin' him fail my daughter and call it fatherhood.

From that day forward, I stopped chasin' him for help he never gave.

Stopped beggin' him to step up.

Stopped waitin' for him to become the father I wished he could be.

It was terrifyin' at first, the thought of raisin' a child with special needs completely on my own.

The weight of it felt like too much for one person to carry.

But in a strange way, it was also freein.'

No more rollercoaster of false hope.

No more anxiety every time the phone rang, wonderin' if he'd show up or disappear.

Just me, my babies, and the road ahead.

The weeks that followed were brutal.

There were nights I fell asleep sittin' up, Niaomy on one side, Celeste on the other, unpaid bills scattered across my lap.

There were mornings when the fridge was almost empty, and I had to stretch one meal into three just to keep us goin.'

I'd cry in the shower so my kids wouldn't see me breakin' down.

But slowly I started buildin' routines.

I learned to budget down to the penny, every dollar planned before it even hit my account.

I found free programs, food banks, and parent groups that understood what I was goin' through.

I learned to ask for help, not from people who wanted to control me or judge me but from those who genuinely wanted to see me and my kids thrive.

Every small victory felt like a mountain climbed..

The first time Niaomy said a full sentence without stutterin.'

The moment we sat down to a full meal I didn't have to borrow money to make happen.

Those wins became my fuel.

It was proof that we were movin' forward, no matter how slow it felt.

One Saturday, I took the kids to the park.

Niaomy ran straight to the swings, laughin,' her curls bouncin' in the sun.

My daughter sat beside me on the bench, carefully linin' up her barbie dolls, hummin' softly to herself.

For a moment, everything felt… normal.

Peaceful.

I closed my eyes and let the sunlight warm my face.

After everything—the fights, the grief, the sleepless nights—here we were.

Still standin.'

Still smilin.'

I whispered to Granny, my voice breakin,' "Look at us. We made it another day."

As spring turned to summer, I started dreamin' again.

About goin' back to school.

About startin' my own business.

About creatin' a life that wasn't just about survivin' but truly livin.'

I knew the road ahead wouldn't be easy.

There would still be challenges, still be nights of tears, and mornings of exhaustion.

But for the first time, I could see a future where the past didn't define me.

My girls deserved that future.

And so did I.

So, I decided to keep walkin.'

One step, one prayer, one breath at a time.

Because even on the hardest days, I knew this much to be true: We were never goin' back to the way things used to be. We were movin' forward, no matter what it took.

CHAPTER SIXTEEN

TRAUMA SURVIVAL

*Choosing life, and crossing a state
line with nothing but faith*

Leavin' Oakland wasn't a choice, it was survival. If I stayed, my daughter would inherit my wounds. I looked at Niaomy and saw a future tryna grow in soil that stayed toxic no matter how much I watered. Tommy's drama, his dysfunctional family, the fake friends, the quiet hate, the loud rumors in every hallway I turned down, the same cycles waited with open arms. I wanted my baby to know soft love, not hard lessons. I wanted breath, not brace.

So, I said a prayer that sounded like a whisper and a war at the same time, and I packed our life into a trunk.

Me and Kameron had two kids and a car. That was it. No savings, no safety net, no couch to crash on. Just two tired people who weren't good together, but stayed solid when it came to survival. We argued plenty, but we moved when it mattered. We loaded the backseat with clothes, diapers, snacks, and that little blanket of Niaomy's she wouldn't sleep without. Celeste clapped at the open road like a game. I tucked fear under my tongue and told God, "Let this be the last time I choose pain over peace."

I stopped clockin' in at jobs that couldn't carry us. And when the money got ugly, I did what I knew—I conversed with men for cash, kept the lights on with words I didn't mean and smiles I couldn't afford. It wasn't pride; it was survival. Some months, my daughter's checks kept us afloat like a life vest I hated needin.' I promised myself it wasn't forever. Just until we crossed some line I couldn't name yet.

International gave way to highways that felt like they'd never end. I watched the city shrink in the rearview and dared my heart not to look back. Granny's voice rode shotgun in my spirit: *Keep pushin,' Pooh.* The girls slept in shifts, and every time the car got quiet, my head filled with all the things that could go wrong: engine heat, flat tires, "what if Texas don't love us either?" I drove anyway. Fear rode in the car. Faith held the wheel.

Texas air felt different like somebody cracked a window in a room I'd been suffocatin' in for years. We found a place. Not fancy, but ours. Four walls that didn't ask where we'd been or what we survived. We set the kids' shoes at the door, put the blanket on the floor, and called it a livin' room. We ate noodles and laughed loud and slept hard. I thought, *maybe this is the start of the soft life I owe my babies.*

At first, the neighbors smiled big. "We family," they said, arms full of furniture and bags of clothes. "We won't tell nobody." Next morning, the whole block knew what they gave us, how much it cost, whose savings they dipped into, which one of us looked "more grateful." I learned quick: fake was bilingual, fluent in hugs and gossip. After that, we kept to ourselves. We brought west coast hustle to southern heat—car, daycare, classes, odd jobs. Survive first. Explain later.

Me and Kameron weren't a fairytale; we were a contract with no witnesses: feed the kids, keep a roof, try again tomorrow. Some days we were a machine tight, efficient, present. Some nights we were strangers on opposite ends of a couch. We didn't make love. We made plans. We didn't daydream. We calculated. When money dried up, I slipped back into conversations-for-cash, hated it, did it anyway, prayed through it. When I could, I worked. When I couldn't, I registered for classes again, chasin' my associates and my bachelor's piece by piece, class by class. I kept tellin' myself, *It's not pretty. It's progress.*

Daycare drop-offs, community college sign-ins, notes scribbled on the backs of grocery lists. I learned the math of stretchin' a dollar, the science of stackin' small wins until they looked like a life. Celeste's giggles in a half-empty apartment felt like wealth money couldn't buy. When Niaomy fell asleep on my chest, I knew I'd done one thing right that day. That had to be enough.

Somewhere between the night shifts and the online quizzes, me and Kameron started splittin' in places we couldn't glue back. We were separated inside the same life—arguin' more, touchin' less, sleepin' next to versions of ourselves we didn't recognize. I didn't say this out loud then, but loneliness made old habits look like new hope. A voice from back home started to sound like comfort. I told myself it was just conversation. I told myself a lot of things. I promised I would not let Texas become a new stage for my old pain. I promised to turn hustle into structure, survival into stability, noise into degree plans, and business paperwork with my name on top. I promised to try the kind of love that started with me even if I didn't know how to keep it yet.

I didn't know I'd conceive my son here. I didn't know the world would shut down and the walls would press in. I didn't know help could look like harm in a uniform or that I'd have to learn to defend my life with my voice in a dean's office. I didn't know Texas would ask me, over and over: *Who are you becoming, Amber?*

Leavin' Oakland wasn't runnin'; it was choosin' life.

CHAPTER SEVENTEEN

BADGES & ACCUSATIONS

How Texas smiled in my face and still tried to make me a suspect.

We had just sat down in that community college classroom—me with my notebook open, tryna act like sleep wasn't chasin' me from the night before. Kameron was two doors down in his class. I told myself, *new state, new start. Do the work. Keep your head down.* I was really tryin.'

The door swung open. Two officers. Whole room froze. "Amber Crown?"

My stomach dropped like a trap door. Everybody looked at me like I'd brought trouble from Oakland in my backpack. I stood up slow, lips pressed together. I heard someone whisper, "Damn."

They walked me into the hall. Then they brought Kameron out, too. We weren't even in the same class, and they still made a show out of it like we were some kind of duo in a crime show.

The first one talked like he practiced soundin' calm. "Ma'am, you're not in trouble. We just need to ask a few questions. You match the description of a suspect who broke into the women's locker room and stole a computer."

"Match the description how?" I asked, already feelin' heat crawl up my neck.

"She had black and burgundy hair."

I blinked. "So… all Black girls with burgundy hair look alike now?"

The sergeant next to him shifted like my words made his boots too tight. "We didn't say that," he snapped.

"You didn't have to," I said.

They added a Big 5 robbery to the story, said we looked like the people involved. Then they *showed* me the girl. And listen, God as my witness, she was bigger than me, darker than me, face nothin' like mine. Only thing we shared was a hair color you could buy at any beauty supply.

"You said it looks like you," the sergeant claimed.

"I never said that," I replied, steady. "I said y'all think we all look the same."

His face changed.

After that day, we were watched. Not "security walking by" watched. I mean watched. Eyes on me in the library. Eyes on me at the vendin' machine. Eyes on me when I signed in, signed out, walked to the bathroom, walked back. I felt it on my shoulder blades like a hand I didn't consent to.

They went through our info like they were scannin' barcodes. Asked Kameron if he'd been to pawn shops. What that got to do with a locker room? Brought up "histories," tried to make poverty sound like proof.

I went home that night and cried in the shower so the kids wouldn't hear my voice breakin.' I told God, *if this state is gonna be a new life, then show me how to fight soft—smart—not with fists but with truth.*

A week later, I was walkin' across campus with a classmate, laughin' about nothin,' tryna pretend my shoulders ain't been tight for days when a pack of police academy students came at us fast. Like a drill. Like they'd been waitin' to pounce.

"Ma'am! Ma'am! We got calls. They said it's you. We need you to come with us."

My classmate stepped back, eyes wide. I stood still. I was done runnin' from anybody's mouth.

"First of all," I said. "You're training, not sworn. And second, they said is no evidence."

One of them looked extra hyped like he wanted to earn a gold star. "I swear to God, people are calling. They said it was you."

"You swore to God and still lyin'," I told him. "Y'all said I got into a white car the other day. I don't even drive a white car. Mine is silver. So, which is it? Y'all can't even keep your story straight."

He opened and closed his mouth like a porch door in wind.

"Listen," I said, voice calm but cuttin' sharp. "You're embarrassin' me in public, you're harassin' a student with no proof, and you keep changin' details to make me fit your picture. That's racism, whether you dress it in a uniform or a syllabus."

Silence. Even the air paused to hear me.

I went to the president's office. Didn't wait for another show outside the classroom. I walked in with my back straight and my heart punchin' my ribs, and I told the whole story to the president and his assistant. I told it clean. Dates, times, who said what. I said I would not be dragged on this campus again for a crime I did not commit.

They pulled footage. They looked at the pictures. They looked at me.

"That's not you," the assistant said, shakin' her head. "Not the same build, not the same face."

The president nodded slow. "We agree."

They filed the complaint themselves. Wrote it up strong. "We can't speak for how it'll be received," they warned. "But we stand with you."

I walked out fightin' tears, half from anger, half from relief. I kept whisperin', "God, cover me," under my breath like armor.

A couple days later, my phone rang. President's office. "It went in your favor," he said. "You will not be bothered again."

I sat on the edge of the bed and finally let the tears come. Not weak tears release. My babies played in the next room like the world wasn't tryna rewrite their mama as a suspect.

I thanked him. I thanked God louder.

This ain't the story I wanted when I crossed that state line. I thought Texas meant soft starts and quiet mornings. Instead, the state smiled, then showed me its teeth. I learned quick: geography didn't save you. Systems traveled. Bias didn't need a passport.

That day, I chose another kind of fight. Paperwork over panic. Names, dates, witnesses, memory like a blade. I promised myself I'd never let anybody paint me guilty just because my skin matched their fear.

People loved to call us "angry Black women." They didn't care what the uniform said to us first. They didn't ask what stereotypes were put on our backs before we ever did a thing wrong. They didn't ask how many times we swallowed it to survive.

I could've been a headline. I could've been a hashtag. But God.

I walked back onto that campus with my head up, not because it didn't hurt, but because it did. Because my babies needed to see that truth had a spine. Because the next girl after me deserved a hallway that didn't turn into a lineup every time she wore her hair how she liked.

They thought they could make me a suspect. I decided to be a student and a witness of myself, for my people, for my kids.

Texas tried to tell me who I was. I corrected it.

I didn't know the next storm waitin' had a due date. I didn't know I'd be holdin' my own breath in an operatin' room, beggin' God to make a silent room loud. I didn't know the world would shut down and my body would become a battle I barely recognized.

But I knew this: whatever came next, I'd meet it standin.'

CHAPTER EIGHTEEN

THE HUSTLE PLUS THE CALLING

How the world shut down while my body opened to bring Sincere in.

The world was shuttin' down just as my body was openin' up to bring life into it. Sirens on the news, masks on faces, shelves empty like the apocalypse snuck in through the back door. I watched Texas slow to a crawl, and I felt my stomach twist part fear, part morning sickness, part *how we gon' do this again?* I didn't plan another pregnancy. But when I felt him there, small and sure, somethin' in me softened and squared up at the same time.

Two lines. I stared until my eyes burned. I put the stick down, picked it back up, laughed and cried in the same breath. "Sincere," I whispered before I even had the right to name him. "If you're comin,' we gon' make room." I was emotional and nervous, full of love already, even with my knees shakin.' I wanted to be ready. I wasn't. I chose him anyway.

Pandemic rules turned our house into a ship at sea. No visitors. No village. Groceries on porches, elbows instead of hugs. I wiped doorknobs like rituals. The kids learned numbers on cracked tablets. I learned to pray with the news on mute. Kameron was there physically present, tryin' in his way but the air between us carried things we didn't have words for. We tag-teamed the kids, the chores, the lists. Some nights we were teammates. Some nights we were just two tired people breathin' in the same room.

I threw up damn near every day. Not cute nausea—*body-wrung-out* sick. Food wouldn't stay down. Water betrayed me. I lost weight I didn't have to spare, hands on the counter, forehead to the cool cabinet door, tellin' myself, "Breathe, Amber, you gotta breathe." I kept movin' between the couch and the bathroom like it was a commute. When I could eat, it was saltines and little sips like my appetite was learnin' to walk again.

When the doctor said "cerclage," my hands went cold. Again. Third time. I nodded like a soldier takin' orders. I knew what it meant: stitch the gate and guard the miracle. I prayed on the exam table, palms open, whisperin,' "Hold, Lord. Hold him steady. Hold me together." The room smelled like sanitizer with hummin' machines. I stared at ceilin' tiles and counted them like beads, imaginin' each square was one more week Sincere would be safe inside me.

Days blurred into weeks. I learned the rhythm of his feet—little taps that turned to rolls; rolls that turned to stretches that stole my breath. Every kick reminded me there was a God who built men out of heartbeat and hope. I'd lay on my side, palm to belly, and talked to him. "You hear, Mama? We almost there, king. You're wanted. You're chosen. You're protected." I didn't talk about the fear out loud, but I folded it into those blessings and hoped he only heard the light.

Appointments felt like missions. Temperature checks at the door, nurses' eyes tired above their masks. I listened to instructions and read between the lines: "Be careful," "We don't know," "We're trying." I packed my hospital bag early, slid my ID into the front pocket like a shield. Kameron kept the car gassed and the route in his head, quiet but ready.

They wheeled me in under lights that hummed like fluorescent bees. Cold air on warm skin. The nurse squeezed my hand gloved, gentle. "You okay, Amber?"

"I'm here," I said, voice steady and small at once. I was awake. Aware. Dizzy around the edges, but present. The anesthesiologist spoke in calm paragraphs; I nodded on the important parts. I felt pressure, heard metal clanking, smelled that clean-clinical nothin' that made you remember every prayer you ever prayed.

Time stretched. The blue drape was a wall between what I knew and what I feared. "You're doing great," a voice said. I focused on a spot in the ceilin' and made a deal with God: if You bring him out breathing, I'll spend the rest of my life showin' him how to use that breath.

Then the room got quiet. Too quiet. I didn't see him, but I heard movement shift, fast hands, the kind of silence that was louder than a scream. My heart pounded so hard it felt like I was shakin' the table. I swallowed air.

I didn't hear a cry.

Suction.

A small wet sound.

Another suction.

Then the crisp pop of a slap, firm and sure once, twice like someone knockin' on a door I couldn't reach.

"Come on, baby," I whispered, voice crackin.' "Come on, Sincere."

Another suction. The longest half-second of my life unfolded and sat on my chest.

Then there it was.

High and bright and brand-new Sincere found his voice and tore the quiet open. The nurse laughed out loud, a sweet sound I'll remember when I'm ninety. "He's beautiful," somebody said. "Look at him."

My eyes flooded so fast I could taste salt. "I love you," I said over and over, the words tumblin' out like they'd been waitin' behind my teeth for months. "Mama loves you. You hear me? I love you."

They brought him close enough for me to see his face—warm, perfect, and angry at the air like all kings were when they first arrived. I kissed the space the mask would allow, reached for his tiny hand, and he curled a finger like he already knew me.

The room was still. The world was still the world. But in that moment, everything changed anyway.

And I held on.

CHAPTER NINETEEN

BECOMING THE WOMAN I PRAYED FOR

Redefining success, healing for real, and embracing everything God said I could be.

The evening sky laid itself down soft, all peaches and gold like God was paintin' peace across the day. My kids' laughter floated through the air—music that reached places therapy hadn't touched yet. Niaomy pumped her legs on the swing like she had a date with the clouds. Celeste chased bubbles barefoot, catchin' them just before they burst like she was savin' tiny worlds. And Sincere sat beside me on the bench, linin' up his little toy cars with that quiet focus only he understood. Every few minutes, he glanced up at me with those deep eyes, and I squeezed his hand. "Mama's here. Always."

Across the playground, Kameron kept quiet watch. We wasn't together, and that was the truth. But we showed up for these kids. That was the mission. That was the assignment. Family didn't always look like the picture but it could still be solid.

Mornings at my house didn't creep; they kicked the door in. Alarms. Lunches. Hair. Shoes nobody could ever find. Sincere hummin' while linin' up his cars on the table. Celeste spinnin' in pajamas, claimin' the livin' room as her dance stage. And my firstborn, the steady one, helpin' her siblings while askin' a million questions about life I was still tryna answer for myself.

I sipped my caramel frappé, don't judge me… that was my gas… and I kept it movin.' School emails, therapy schedules, daycare calls, grocery runs, business plans. Some nights, I fell asleep with the light still on, but sunrise kept findin' me. And I kept showin' up.

People thought Sincere was silent. He was not. He just spoke love in his own dialect. When the world gets loud, he pressed his forehead to mine and breathed with me until it slowed down. Some days in therapy, he shut down and stared through walls. Other days, he stacked blocks like an architect God trained Himself. Every small win was a holiday in our home.

One night, I told him, "Baby, you don't need words for me to understand you. I see you. Mama hears you."

Celeste was a firework with no warnin' label. She climbed high, jumped far, laughed loud, and loved big. I protected that spark like it was family inheritance because it was.

And Niaomy? She carried Granny's spirit like an heirloom. Wise eyes. Old soul. Heart too loyal for this world. One night, while I braided her hair, she asked, "Mommy, why do you work so much?"

I paused, comb in hand, looked at her through the mirror.

"So you never have to survive like I did. I want you to inherit options, not wounds."

People sent things every blue moon. But we learned not to wait for help that came with strings or an expiration date. We didn't have a village. We became the village.

Me and Kameron? We weren't soulmates, but we were teammates for these kids. And sometimes, that was a bigger blessin' than a ring.

We ended the day how we started outside. The sun clocked out slow, the sky dipped lavender. Niaomy called, "Mama, you watching?" Celeste twirled like she owned the air. Sincere hummed his soft little notes and leaned into me, cheek warm on my arm. I wrapped my arms around all three, breathin' them in like medicine.

"Look at us," I whispered. "We're not just survivin' anymore. We're buildin.'"

For the first time, I didn't fear what was comin.' I felt ready for it. All of it.

I didn't become who they said I'd be.

I became who God called me to be

and I'm still becomin.'

For every woman stitchin' herself back together after love tried to unmake her, may your boundaries be blessed, your rest be holy, and your next chapter be soft on your spirit.

If I made it here, you can too.

Keep choosin' you loud, daily, and without apology.

EPILOGUE

I am a Texas mobile notary pull-up service, professional, discreet. I stamp papers with integrity and prayer. I'm also rebranding Modest Royalteez—new designs, new meaning, same mission: **walk with dignity**. And I'm writing books at my kitchen table between bedtime routines and client calls. Not a one-time author either; I got more stories in me, waiting their turn.

And let's be clear, I'm now working on my master's degree after earning my associate's and bachelor's. I'm doing this degree as a mother, as a businesswoman, as a woman who refuses to stay stuck in the life she was handed.

Michelle may be my biological mother, but she wasn't a mother to me, and she ain't a grandmother to my kids. Word around town is she's worn thin, life heavy on her skin. I don't drag her. Life already did. I pray from a distance because I know what abandonment feels like, and I refuse to feed my kids what I had to digest.

My father, Thomas? We talk every few months. Love is there, but so is pride, silence, distance, and unhealed childhood pieces that still bleed if you touch them wrong. I love him. I pray for him. But my peace don't live in his house, so loving him from afar is holy, too.

"Fathers, do not embitter your children, or they will become discouraged," Colossians 3:21 (NIV)

I carry that scripture like a compass. My kids will not inherit the discouragement I carried. The cycle ends with me.

I am single. Six months out of a breakup that could've drowned me if I didn't learn how to float on my own tears. I learned the hard way: being a man's ride-or-die don't earn you trophies. It'll park you at the crime scene of his chaos with the blame on your back. I left the father of my children for someone I *thought* was my person. He wasn't. It wasn't love. It was trauma holding hands with comfort.

Now? I'm dating myself for the first time. I'm filling my own cup before I pour. Therapy, boundaries, journaling, prayer. Candles that smell like soft mornings. I delete messages I don't need to respond to. I don't explain my peace to anybody who wasn't here when I was breaking.

Sometimes self-love is loud. Sometimes it's quiet. Most days, it's work. But it's my work now.

Legacy Work

Our home has a new language. We speak "I'm proud of you" daily. We celebrate the small things: a new word from Sincere, a good grade from Niaomy, Celeste sleeping through the night without a nightmare. We rest. We laugh. We heal in public, so they never think healing is shameful.

I want generational wealth for them but before money, I want generational peace. I want my kids to inherit love that doesn't leave scars, faith that doesn't require survival mode, joy that doesn't need permission.

Modest Royalteez is leveling up pieces that speak life, clothing with identity, hood royalty on fabric. I notarize paperwork at kitchen tables and porches, praying silently for the people signing. And I write because my story is turning into somebody else's survival guide.

I talk to Granny when I wash dishes. I feel her when I'm tired but keep going anyway. She never met Celeste or Sincere, but her fingerprints are on how I mother them. Her love didn't die; it multiplied.

I hear her every time quitting tries to flirt with me, *"Keep pushing, Pooh. You were built for this."*

And I whisper back, "I know. Thank you."

I stopped waiting for someone to choose me. I chose **me**. I stopped begging for support from people who liked me better broken. I stopped shrinking to fit friendships that didn't clap when I healed.

I'm not perfect. I'm present. I'm not healed all the way. I'm healing out loud.

I'm raising children who know they matter.

I'm building a business with my name on it.

I'm earning my master's after completing my associate's and bachelor's.

I'm becoming a woman my younger self needed.

Becoming the woman I prayed for didn't look like magic; it looked like discipline, tears, breaking, boundaries, surrender, and believing God when nobody else believed in me.

REFLECTION LETTER

Sometimes silence speaks the loudest.

After everything I've lived through, witnessed, and survived. One thing I've learned is this: you can't force people to understand your pain if they were never built to carry it. I used to try to explain myself to folks who never cared to listen. I used to beg for apologies, closure, or honesty from people who had already decided they would never give it.

And still, I gave love. Still, I forgave. Still, I held space in my heart for people who threw salt in my wounds.

But no more.

I look back now and realize it wasn't just what people said, it was all the shit they didn't do. This letter isn't to the ones who broke me. It's not even for the ones who stayed. This is for me. The version of me that kept going. The girl who cried in silence and wiped her own tears. The woman who still rose when life tried to bury her.

I don't need validation anymore. I don't need the whole world to know if I was right or wrong. I just need peace. And healing. And God. And I got all three now.

So, this is my final reflection, one not rooted in revenge, but in release. I'm still learning. Still healing. Still growing. But I finally understand and show up for the woman I see in the mirror. She survived everything meant to destroy her.

ACKNOWLEDGMENTS

I would like to thank my grandmother, Ruby Jean Hamilton, for helping my father raise me even when he wasn't always present. She saved me from a lot of trouble and teenage pregnancy, kept me in school, and showed up for every milestone in my life for twenty-three years. Up until her passing, I wasn't always easy to deal with, but her love was undeniably real. I will forever love you, Granny.

To my kids, thank you for keeping me and going through the uncertainty on the bad days and the good ones. Your love is unwavering, and God knew I needed you.

To my children's father, thank you for not giving up on me even after our separation. It was a failed relationship, but not a failed co-parenting journey. You helped where you didn't have to, and that means something.

Thank you to the people who hurt me and taught me lessons through pain. To the ones I've forgiven, and the ones I'm still learning to forgive, every wound shaped this story.

A special thank you to my editor, Ashley Mustafaa, for your support and encouragement. Your editorial skills are outstanding, and your voice has been both valuable and necessary for my work. You deserve your flowers.

Lastly, thank you to the person reading this memoir who sees themselves in these pages.

Keep going, girl.

God is not finished with you yet.

Take this—my words, my voice—and let it remind you that healing is still possible.

You matter.

You're not alone.

Make it great.

ABOUT THE AUTHOR

Amber Westbrooks is a devoted mother of three beautiful children and a proud resident of Houston, Texas. She is currently pursuing her graduate degree at Stephen F. Austin State University with an anticipated graduation in May 2026 to earn her master's degree. *Fail to See* marks her debut as an author; a deep and personal journey told through raw honesty, resilience, and faith in her own growth.

In addition to her writing, Amber is an emerging entrepreneur and the founder of Modest Royalteez, a clothing brand created to inspire self-love, self-worth, and spiritual richness. Her mission is to spark a positive movement that reminds people they are greater than the circumstances they were born into or the limitations others have placed on them. Through her brand and her words, she encourages others to take control of their journey, discover the beauty in it, and strive toward becoming their highest self.

Amber's life has been shaped by both triumphs and trials. She grew up without her mother's presence, had an on-and-off relationship with her father, and never lived with her biological siblings despite having connections with them throughout the years. She is a survivor of domestic violence and sexual assault, and her past has left deep impacts on her interpersonal relationships. Along the way, she has made mistakes but she has also done deep self-reflection and committed herself to making better decisions.

Amber describes her current season as a *complete healing journey*. She grew up tough, and that toughness has carried her through some of life's most difficult storms. To know her is to love her because behind her strength is a woman determined to heal, inspire, and help others see that their story is still worth writing.

Made in the USA
Coppell, TX
27 February 2026

72545131R00121